S0-CGP-801

FINDING TRUE LOVE

FINDING TRUE LOVE

•

Shelley Galloway

AVALON BOOKS
NEW YORK

Library of Congress Catalog Card Number: 2002090724
ISBN 0-8034-9545-5

Published by Thomas Bouregy & Co., Inc.
160 Madison Avenue, New York, NY 10016

PRINTED IN THE UNITED STATES OF AMERICA
ON ACID-FREE PAPER
BY HADDON CRAFTSMEN, BLOOMSBURG, PENNSYLVANIA

To my family, who remind me daily that I am loved.

Special thanks to the Loveland Historical Society, my writing buddy, Heather, and my friend Beth, who told me a really great story one afternoon . . . and graciously allowed me to share it.

Chapter One

W*ell, what now?* Missy thought to herself. She tried not to panic as her car came to a grinding halt on the shoulder of Interstate 275, after lurching for a few feet in short, desperate bursts. She looked out the window and sighed.

Driving in the pouring rain was no problem. Even driving in the rain at two in the morning was doable. But having the car run out of gas, in the rain, at two in the morning, on the side of the freeway, with no cell phone, was more than she could take. What was she going to do?

Glumly, she looked out her window. Between the darkness and the pelting rain, there really wasn't much to see. The freeway light erected ten yards ahead didn't help much. Shadows of cars, blurry headlights, and the ominous presence of the huge semis as they roared by were the only objects she could make out.

A chill passed through her. She felt vulnerable, alone. She closed her eyes for a brief moment. What was she going to do?

Missy forced herself to think clearly and take note of her circumstances. She was probably ten miles from home. If she remembered correctly, the next exit was at least another two miles farther down the road. There seemed to be nothing to do except turn on her hazards and wait—for what, she didn't know.

This was truly the final touch to a really bad day. Not only had she had to work late at the historical museum, but then she had naively volunteered to go represent the museum at a meeting in downtown Cincinnati. Then Kathleen, the volunteer who had intended to go with her, couldn't make the meeting. She had been forced to go to the meeting alone. And she hated driving on the highway at night.

Missy stared out the window, then glanced at the digital clock on her dash. Twenty minutes had passed.

The early March air was chilly. She pulled her coat closer around her. The rain hammered against her car in staccato beats. There was really nothing to do but wait, and perhaps pray.

She was forced out of her thoughts by the appearance of a sedan suddenly pulling up behind her, its outline blurred in the glare from its headlights. She quickly looked for signs that it was a police car, but didn't see strobe lights or an antenna—only the dark figure of a man in a slicker getting out of the car and walking toward her.

Missy looked around her and slowly shrank into the seat. The same question surfaced again in her head: What was she going to do?

She peeked out the driver's side mirror. The street light cast a hazy shadow around the man as he approached. He looked huge in the rain. All she could discern was a light colored baseball cap, a yellow slicker, and a quick glimpse of pale eyes.

She swallowed nervously, then jumped as the man knocked on her window. Missy forced herself to look straight ahead.

"Ma'am?" she heard him say, muffled through the barriers of rain and glass. "Do you need some help?"

Missy drew in another tense breath. Suddenly, every warning she had ever heard about taking help from strangers came to mind. Sensing he was waiting for a reply, she shook her head.

A crash of thunder reverberated in the distance.

After a pause, the man knocked again. "It's pretty bad out here. You don't want to be sitting like a target on the side of the road." His words were cut off as he stepped aside. The roar of an eighteen-wheeler approached, then the lumbering truck passed, spraying water in its wake.

Missy forced herself to look straight ahead.

"Can I give you a hand?" he shouted.

Maybe it was the yellow slicker, maybe it was the realization that he seemed determined to stay out there, getting soaked by the trucks, but after another few seconds, Missy turned to look at him.

Their eyes met through the glass barrier, hers wide and frightened, his calm and concerned. "I'm out of gas," she called to him.

He nodded, then visibly tensed as another truck came up behind them. He held up a hand, indicating that he was going to the passenger side, away from the oncoming cars. Once there, he spoke again, shouting. "Where you headed?"

"Payton," she called out.

He looked at her quizzically. "Where?"

The rain was coming down hard. "Payton," she said, louder.

The man looked around him, seemed to judge the conditions, then made a motion for her to roll her window down.

Those stranger-danger stories came back in a flash. The glass was the only thing between her and the man. She shook her head. "No."

Their eyes met again. The man opened his mouth for a moment, then held up a hand and walked away.

Missy watched him walk behind her car to his, and immediately felt a sense of loss. "Fool," she muttered to herself. "You're going to have to trust somebody, sometime." Suddenly the company of the stranger felt much better than being alone. She glanced at her watch. Three A.M. She clasped her hands closer to her body. They felt cold even through the fabric of her suit. She rubbed them against her thighs, trying to restore warmth to her fingers.

When she lifted her head again, the man was back, but this time, he was armed with a crowbar. She closed her eyes tightly, but her eyes had already welled with tears. "Oh my God," she muttered. "Is he going to break my window? Should I honk my horn?" Her eyes darted to the doors. They were locked.

The man knocked again on the passenger window and again made a motion for her to unroll the window.

She shook her head.

"Just a little? An inch?" he yelled, his thumb and index finger close together.

Missy was cold, her body was shaking from fear, and she knew she was about to break down and start crying in earnest any minute. But through the haze, she realized that if he was going to smash in the glass, he would have already done so. It took every ounce of courage she had to push the button and lower the glass an inch. Immediately, cold rain flew inside, spraying the fabric of her coat.

The man leaned down, his mouth close to the opening. In the dim light, his eyes looked warm. "Look, I know you're scared, and I know you don't trust me, but at least let me call the police for you." He pulled a cell phone out of the pocket of his slicker.

"All right." She lowered the glass two more inches.

"What's your name?" he asked, already dialing the number.

"Missy Schuler."

He looked at her quizzically. "I'm Kevin Reece."

His name was familiar. She tried to place it as she heard him practically shout into the phone.

"No, there's no accident."

"Yes, but . . ."

"All right . . . thanks."

He turned to her. "The storm's pretty bad. It knocked out the power on the western half of Payton. Plus there was a pretty bad accident. They say it's going to be a while."

"How long?"

He shrugged. "They couldn't say. Maybe half an hour? Forty-five minutes. . . ." He sighed. "Can I just give you a lift home? I live in Payton too."

She knew he was soaking wet. She also knew that because Payton had such a small police force, he was probably telling the truth. How could she depend on him? "I'm fine."

He pursed his mouth. "Look," he said again as he leaned down and picked up the crowbar. "How about this: I slide this crowbar to you, then you get out of the car and let me drive you home. I'll give you my phone to hold too. If I do anything that you think I shouldn't, you can hit me with it and call the police yourself. All right?"

The rain came down harder and blew into the car.

Missy studied his expression. There was something familiar about his eyes, though she couldn't say exactly what.

Suddenly, all Missy knew was that she was exhausted and she wanted to get home. She was going to have to trust somebody. There had to be some men in this world who were decent. "All right."

The man's body seemed to relax. "Great." He smiled, sliding the crowbar and phone through the crack in the window.

Missy grasped the cold wet metal, then held it firmly in her hands. It was heavier than it looked, but did indeed give her confidence. "Let me get my things."

"I'll go turn on my car. I'd go out this side, if I were you," he said, then walked towards the sedan behind her.

After rolling up her window and grabbing her bag and purse, Missy slid over to the passenger side, grasped the crowbar and phone, and climbed out of the car. Rain pelted her, the shock of the freezing sleet making her gasp. Tentatively, she began to follow the stranger.

As soon as she reached the car, the man leaned across and opened the passenger side for her. Cautiously, she stepped in and closed the door. The heater was on full blast and instantly brought comfort.

"I'm glad you decided to trust me," the man said as she buckled up and placed the crowbar and phone across her lap, still holding the metal bar tight. "It was getting pretty cold out there."

She forced herself to reply, to remain calm. "Thank you for stopping."

"No problem." He pulled out into traffic. "Well, like I said, my name's Kevin Reece."

Finally she was able to place the name. She relaxed her grip on the crowbar. That's why his eyes looked familiar. He was her boss's brother. "And I'm Missy Schuler."

"This probably sounds funny, but I've heard your name before . . . I just can't place it."

Missy nodded. "Your sister became the director of the historical museum not too long ago. I work for her as her assistant."

"Oh, yeah." He nodded. "But, I think I had heard it before that. Did you go to Payton High?"

"Yes. I graduated six years ago."

"Small world." The corners of his eyes crinkled as he grinned. "You were two years behind me. Well, I guess from Joanne you know that there's five of us. I've been working so much, I haven't had time to visit Joanne much. Do you know my brothers or Denise?"

She knew *of* them. Everyone knew of the Reece kids. Missy looked around the car, wondering what to say . . . that she knew of his family but they didn't run in the same social circles?

Suddenly she became aware of the leather interior of the Lexus, of Kevin's designer shirt. She swallowed hard. "Well, I've heard of the Reece kids, but that's about it."

"With so many to live up to, I think every teacher had at least one story for me about a sibling." Reece smiled.

"I think we had a class together once. Did you ever take French?" Missy asked.

"French I, as a junior." He replied.

"I took it as a freshman. I remember that you always found a way to leave early."

"That class was tough for me because I had football right after, and the coach wanted us on the field within five minutes of the bell ringing. Monsieur Girard's class was on the opposite side of campus." He paused a moment, looking at her thoughtfully. "I don't recall much about that class, other than I hated it. But I do remember you, I think. Didn't you have thick glasses and a lot of hair?"

She laughed. "Yep, that pretty much sums up my appearance as a freshman. You were nice though. One time you gave me a pencil and paper and let me share your book when I had forgotten my backpack at home."

Kevin glanced at her again. "Small world, huh?" he said again.

Missy nodded as she stole a glance at his profile. Even in the dim light she could see his dark blond hair peeking out from under his cap, the unusual gray eyes—eyes that looked as if a ring of blue or green bordered the edges—and his thick, almost brown eyebrows. Strong jaw. Large hands with his nails trimmed short. “I was an only child,” she said, mainly as an excuse to fill the silence that hung between them.

Kevin guided the car off the freeway at the Payton exit. “Where to?”

She glanced at him again. There was just something so friendly about him. He seemed nothing like Scott. Then she realized he was waiting for a reply. “Um, I live off Main Street.” As soon as she said the words, she waited for a derisive comment. The homes off Main were known to be in the lowest priced section of town.

When he only nodded, her hands released the crowbar. “I know it’s none of my business, but what were you doing out at three A.M. in this storm?” she asked, before she thought better of it.

“I was downtown with some friends tonight. We’re celebrating my promotion.”

“Oh, a promotion?” For lack of anything else to say, she added, “What do you do?”

“Well, as of last week, I am the regional director for Consolidated Industries.”

Everyone knew that Consolidated was one of the fastest growing companies in the city. They not only manufactured engines, but also had divisions in a half-dozen other areas. Missy knew automatically that for Kevin to be working there, it was a very good job. “Wow,” she said inanely.

He only smiled in response. "Okay. We're on Main. Now where?"

"Take the third right." She continued to give him directions until they stopped in front of a duplex. "This is me," she said, pointing to the right side of a white clapboard building.

Kevin parked the car, then turned to face her. "Hey, didn't I hear something about you getting married to Scott Hawkins?"

Missy bit her lip. "We did get married, but . . . it didn't work out. We were only married for ten months."

Kevin's features became etched with concern, and Missy could see a line of questioning in his eyes. She didn't know why she felt obligated to tell him more, but she did. "Scott moved away when I, ah, left him. I did odd jobs for a few years after that . . . but then I took some night school classes at the community college and then got the job at the museum."

"Do you like working there?"

"Oh, sure."

He grinned. "How's Joanne? Is she still a mess?"

"You're speaking like a brother! For your information, Joanne is great," she said loyally. "She's done a lot of good things for Payton."

Kevin chuckled. "You're right. I just like to give her a hard time, I guess."

She realized abruptly that it was time to go. "Thanks

again. I truly don't know what I would have done without your help."

"Anytime," he said, glancing at her place.

Missy winced as she tried to see it through his eyes. The paint was dull, and the bushes that lined the front were raggedy. It was obvious that she was still struggling to make ends meet.

"What about your car?"

She closed her eyes. It had been so good to pretend for a moment that she had no cares, that she was getting dropped off from a date, not just delivered home. "I'll have someone help me take care of it in the morning." She glanced at her watch. Three-thirty. "Well, in a few hours."

"Do you have family in town?"

"Oh, no. I'm all alone." Missy's eyes widened as she realized how pitiful that sounded. "I mean, I'll get a friend to help me out."

"I'll be glad to help you. It's Saturday. How about I come to get you around eleven? It will give us some time to sleep, but not leave your car out too long?"

What could she say? He had already done more than enough. "No, thanks. I'll be fine."

"Are you still afraid of me?"

She swallowed again. "No, but I hate to be trouble."

He reached out, gently pulled the crowbar from her lap, and set it on the floor near her feet. "It's no trouble." He flashed her a smile. "Anyway, Joanne would have my head if I didn't help you."

What was it about him that inspired trust? "Thank you. That's very kind of you." There seemed to be nothing else to say. She unbuckled, then reached behind her to get her purse and tote bag.

Kevin had already opened his door and was walking around to her side.

"I'm fine," she said as he pulled open her door.

"I know," he replied simply after they began to walk towards her front door. The rain pelted them both as he walked her to the shabby entrance of her home.

She reached in her bag for her key, slid it into the lock, and turned the latch. He was still there. She cleared her throat. "Thanks again."

He still stood in the rain as she stepped over the threshold. "Turn on a light, Missy."

She did automatically, then blushed. The illuminated room only served to accentuate her lack of furniture. "I . . . ," she began.

But Kevin only reached towards her and brushed her forearm gently. "I'll see you later, Missy Schuler. Get some sleep." He turned away and strode back to his car.

Missy closed the door behind her and leaned against it for a moment. What a night. What a crazy, mixed-up, scary, wonderful night. Not only had she had one of the worst things ever happen to her in months, but she also felt alive again, for the first time in years. It was if meeting Kevin Reece had reawakened her senses.

She climbed the stairs to her bedroom, changed into her flannel nightgown, and brushed her teeth on autopilot. But when she climbed into bed, she thought of Kevin. Of Joanne. Of the whole Reece family. Of how she had felt about them in high school, so long ago. The rich, popular kids for whom everything had always seemed so easy.

Missy closed her eyes, remembering. Joanne had been homecoming queen. Kevin, the quarterback on the football team. Another had graduated as valedictorian. All were known to be friendly and nice.

And Joanne *was* nice, and fun to work for, she reminded herself.

But back in high school, Joanne and her crowd had seemed so far away. Missy hadn't even known her well enough to say hi. She hadn't gone to the parties or to the dances that Joanne had. She had been too quiet, too poor. Well, she had been nice, she corrected herself, but so shy that no one even noticed her. Except Scott. But all he had ever done was break her heart.

Now Kevin was going to pick her up tomorrow to get her car. He had walked her to her door. He had made her feel special, like a real person. Missy smiled. It was a good feeling, to feel noticed again. It was worth savoring.

Finally, at four A.M., she slept.

Chapter Two

Kevin arrived at his parents' house the next day ready for a decent breakfast and information. His mom, a textbook morning person, had a habit of making breakfast on Saturday mornings and assuming a few of her children would stop by to join her. It didn't matter that her children were all in their twenties and living on their own. It was a rare weekend when none of her kids stopped by.

Kevin figured it was a good time to check in with everybody and catch up on news. It would also be a good time to find out some news too. If he wasn't mistaken, his sister Joanne was going to be there, and he wanted to learn more about Missy Schuler.

He entered the old ranch house and immediately felt a sense of comfort. His parents had lived in the same house for as long as he could remember. "Hi, Mom," he called out as he strode toward the kitchen.

He heard several voices coming from the breakfast nook. It looked as if Joanne was already there, as well as a few others. When he entered the room, he saw that not only had he and Joanne decided to come over, but Stratton, Joanne's husband, was there as well. His mom and dad were sitting on the bar stools that lined the counter, sipping coffee and laughing about a story that Stratton was telling.

Kevin gently squeezed his mother's shoulder as he helped himself to a cup of coffee. "Hi, dear," she said, her blue eyes bright. "I didn't know you were going to stop by today."

"What, and miss breakfast?" he teased, before continuing his greetings to the rest of the occupants in the room. "How are y'all doing today?"

Joanne answered. "Just fine. Stratton actually closed the office today, except for emergencies. For once, we've got a whole day to spend together."

"How's work?"

"It's fine too, except that things have been pretty busy. The museum's great, though. But, like I was telling everybody, it's kind of nice to have a Saturday morning to ourselves right now. They really are few and far between."

"We even slept in until eight this morning," Stratton added.

Jim, Kevin's dad, spoke then. "I'm about to play a few rounds of golf. You want to join me?"

This was as good a time as any to share his story and find out some information. "I'm sorry, Dad, but I can't. Something happened last night."

Immediately looks of concern played across everyone's features. "Are you okay?" his mother asked.

Kevin sat down. "I'm fine. It's just that I had an eventful evening last night. When I was driving home from downtown in the rain. . . ."

Already his mother looked as if she was prepared for the worst. "Kevin, you got in a wreck?"

He held up a hand to prevent another question. "No, Mom. I noticed a car pulled over on the side of the road, with a girl in it."

Joanne leaned forward, eyes bright with curiosity. "And—"

"I pulled over and decided to see if I could help."

"What time was this?" Jim asked.

"About three in the morning."

Daphne sighed. "Kevin, haven't you heard how dangerous that can be? What if she had pulled out a gun or something?"

Joanne grinned. "I thought only women were supposed to worry about that happening."

"Not in this day and age," Daphne replied.

Kevin listened to the interplay and realized he should have known he would get treated to everyone's opinion. He spoke fast, before the conversation went off on a trail that he wouldn't be able to follow. "The woman didn't have a gun, guys. She was scared. In fact, it actually took a few minutes to get her to even talk to me. I had to slide a crowbar through the top of a window before she would."

Joanne smiled. "I would have liked to have seen that."

"What happened then?" Stratton inquired.

"Turns out, she was out of gas, and she lives right here in Payton. I went ahead and offered her a ride home."

"Always the Good Samaritan," Joanne said blithely.

His mother jumped to his defense. "I don't think there's anything wrong with that, Joanne."

"I'm just saying that if anyone would fall for the damsel in distress routine, it would be Kevin."

He didn't like the way that sounded. "Hey, I don't think it was a routine. . . ."

His mother, of course, had to share the information she had learned from the previous week's round of talk shows. And that was followed by Jim adding what he'd read in the paper about picking up hitchhikers.

Kevin sipped his coffee patiently and waited until he had their attention again. When they looked ready to listen, he continued. "I dropped her off and promised to take her to get gas and fill up her tank at eleven."

"Don't you think she's taking advantage of your

good nature, Kevin?" his dad asked. "I mean, you've already done enough."

"It wasn't like that, Dad. I had to coax her to let me drive her home, then do the same to let me help her get gas."

Jim coughed. "I can imagine. . . ."

Kevin cut him off. "Besides, it turns out that she wasn't really a stranger—not much of one, anyway. She works for you, Joanne."

That got her attention. "Really? Who was it?"

"Missy Schuler."

Surprise, then recognition, spread across her features. "Oh, thank goodness you were there."

Stratton nodded. "She's a sweet girl. I bet she was scared to death."

"Wow. I'm surprised she took you up on your offer for help. She keeps pretty much to herself."

"Yeah?"

Joanne nodded. "She's sweet as can be, but she's had a rough time of it."

"I thought you liked her."

"Oh, I do. She's helped me a lot, and she's a great worker; she's just had her share of problems, that's all."

"Why would you say that?"

"She's pretty shy at work."

"I've met her, dear, and talked with her several times," their mother said. "She's lovely, and seems like a good-natured girl."

"Oh, she is," Joanne agreed. "I guess I'm saying these things because I've known her, at least slightly, for years. We were in the same graduating class in high school."

Kevin nodded. "I thought so."

Jim narrowed his eyes at his daughter's careful wording. "I've never met her—what's she like?"

"Fragile, I guess." Joanne shrugged. "She never had a lot of money growing up—I think her dad died, or left, or something when we were in junior high. She was always real quiet too, which was funny because she was very pretty. But kids always zeroed in on her shy demeanor, so they never gave her a chance. She was always the type to sit right beside you in class and be so quiet that you would forget she was there."

Joanne looked to her husband for understanding. "About a year after graduation she married that Scott Hawkins."

"She said that's over with," Kevin said.

"I would hope so. Not only was he a really cocky guy in school, but also a bully. A real loser. He was the type who would skip classes and then complain loudly that the teacher was unfair. Most people gave him a pretty wide berth."

"I wonder why Missy ended up with him?" Daphne mused.

"Maybe because he noticed her. I don't know." She pursed her lips. "But I heard he didn't change much after he married Missy." Joanne looked as if she was about to add more, but took a sip of coffee instead.

They were all caught up in Missy's story. "Well?" Stratton prodded. "What happened after they got married?"

Joanne looked uncomfortable. "I guess I shouldn't be spreading this story, but I heard he was mean to her."

Kevin's eyes narrowed. "Mean to her?"

"There were rumors that he always kind of put her down . . . made her do everything . . . but the worst thing I heard was one time when they got into an argument and she fell into a charcoal grill."

Daphne gasped. "Oh my word."

Joanne glanced at her family, concern in her eyes. "I guess she got a few nasty burns. She's got a pretty bad scar on her right arm from it. After that, Scott left town. I think Missy had finally had enough."

"The poor thing," Jim said.

"I hate to say it, but I think it's what she finally needed to take charge of herself. Soon after, she worked as a waitress at The Grill, then in a few department stores during the day, and went to classes at the college at night." Joanne took a sip of coffee. "A few years ago, Mrs. Abrams, the old director of the historical society, hired her to fill in part-time. Now, I have her working full-time."

Joanne turned to her parents. "Missy's wonderful. She gets along well with both the volunteers and the kids who come on tours. I've even been considering asking her to do a few extra projects for the society."

Joanne shook her head. "Of all the people to meet on the side of the road, Kevin, Missy would not have been one I would have thought of." A stricken look crossed her face. "Oh, darn, I bet she was going home from that dumb meeting I asked her to go to. It's all my fault that she was stranded on the road last night!"

Daphne's eyes softened. "No, I think that's just called bad luck, dear." Then she eyed her eldest son for a moment, a calculating look in her eye. "Or fate."

"Or just a funny coincidence," Jim added, his eyes narrowing as he looked at his wife.

Kevin looked at the glances his parents were giving each other and knew it would be best if he just stayed quiet. Besides, there didn't seem much to say. He sipped his coffee and thought about Joanne's story. Kevin couldn't get over the fact that someone had actually harmed that sweet, shy girl he had met.

"Perhaps you should call her up now, see if she wants to come over for breakfast," Daphne offered.

He smiled. Of course his mom would want to feed Missy. Food was her cure for everything. "I don't think so, Mom. I didn't drop her off until almost four. I hope she's sleeping right now."

"I think it's great that you're helping her out, Kevin," his dad said. "Sounds like she was due for some good luck."

Kevin said nothing, only helped himself to a healthy

slice of the cinnamon apple cake that his mother had out, along with a bowl of fruit.

There was something about Missy Schuler that made him want to get to know her better. He glanced at the clock. 10:03. Well, no matter what, in an hour he was due to see her again.

Missy worriedly glanced at the clock. What if he forgot? What if he hadn't really meant to follow through on his promise, or had woken up and decided he had better things to do than to help some girl from the side of the road out again? She got to her feet and glanced out the front window. No, she told herself sternly. He seemed sincere. He was going to come by. And he wouldn't have offered if he hadn't wanted to do this.

She sat down again and examined her outfit: jeans, her best lavender sweater, tan boots. It wasn't fancy, but she knew the jeans flattered her figure, and the lavender color made the blue in her eyes seem brighter. Not that he would notice. But she would. She didn't want his only impression of her to be one formed out of pity.

Missy examined her hands. Her nails were cut short and were unpainted. And of course, her fingers were void of any rings. Perhaps her hands were a good symbol of her state in life right now—simple, no frills. She glanced at her nails again. Even though they weren't painted a bright color, they were filed neatly, and she did take care to rub baby oil on her cuticles every morning. Okay, she corrected herself. Her life might be simple right now, but it was well-kept. That had to count for something, right?

She was saved from further introspection by Kevin's arrival. Her heart quickened. His offer *had* been sincere. As soon as she saw his tan Lexus pull up, she opened the front door. No need for him to have to get out. She was just locking the door when she felt, rather than heard, Kevin's approach.

"Hi," he said simply.

She turned to him. If anything, he looked better than he had the night before. She noticed he had switched his slicker for a thick khaki barn jacket. "Good morning," she answered, then stood dumbly, staring at him. There seemed to be so much more to say, but at the moment she couldn't think of anything.

"You look pretty. Are you feeling better today?"

She blushed. Maybe the care over her outfit had been worth her time and energy. "Thanks, and yes I am. Although I don't think I could have looked any worse last night, soaked from the rain."

She noticed his gaze scan her face. "Were you able to get some sleep?"

"Oh, yes, thanks. I don't think I moved until the alarm went off this morning."

"Alarm? On a Saturday morning?"

"I had a few things I wanted to get done, and there's a bake sale at church I promised to help with. . . ." Her voice drifted off. She had also wanted to look nice when he came for her, but she couldn't really explain that to him. He seemed to be waiting for her to continue, so she asked a question instead. "Uh, did you get some sleep also?"

He smiled. "Sure, but sleeping has never been a problem for me. In college I shared a house with six guys. After living that way for two years, I think I can sleep through anything."

He walked her to the car and held the door open for her, just like a date. But he did it as if he did it all the time, like it was no trouble at all. She settled into the soft leather.

"I guess the first stop we have to make is the gas station," he said. "Do you care which one we go to?"

"Any will do. There's one just down the block."

"All right." They drove in silence for a while. When they approached the station, Missy got out with Kevin, purchased a gasoline can, and proceeded to get a few dollars' worth of gas.

When they were back in his car, she turned to him. "I really want to thank you again for last night, Kevin. I don't know what I would have done. It was so stupid to let my car run out of gas. I'm usually so much more careful than that."

"Don't worry about it. I'm just glad I was there."

"But, you don't know how worried I was. . . ."

He stopped her with a hand that reached out and pressed hers. "Hey, remember my big family? I have two sisters. If either of them ever has car trouble, I hope someone will pull over and help them. It's the right thing to do."

His words effectively stopped her from saying any more about it. She didn't know what it felt like to have a sibling, but she imagined she would feel the same way. They drove in silence for a few more moments. Then, all too soon, they approached her car.

No damage had been done to it in the few hours it had sat there. Kevin pulled up behind it, and then without saying anything, got out, retrieved the gasoline can, and began to fill her tank.

Missy got out and then stood beside him, suddenly feeling at a loss for words. This man was like her knight in shining armor. She had never been around anyone who had such perfect manners, who was so quietly competent. She wondered if he was dating anyone. If so, Missy hoped that the woman knew how lucky she was to have found someone like Kevin Reece.

Missy knew from experience just how few and far between good men were. Images of Scott, with his big plans and no ambition flashed through her mind. He had been coarse and whiny, and worse, she hadn't thought she had deserved better.

"I think you're set," Kevin said then, interrupting her thoughts.

"I . . . great," she said, instead of thanking him for the hundredth time. It was then that she knew she had to gather her courage. She wanted to see this man again. She glanced around. The traffic was light, but the side of the freeway was still no place to begin a conversation. "Uh, can I buy you a cup of coffee, to thank you?"

His gray eyes seemed to warm at her suggestion. "Thanks. I'd like that."

"Have you ever been to that little coffee shop, The Payton Mill?"

"I know it all right. It's about a block away from my brother-in-law's office. I've been there a lot." He paused a moment. "I'll meet you there."

"All right. I'll see you in a few minutes then," Missy said, then unlocked her car door and slid inside. As she turned the key in the ignition, she giggled softly to herself. For the first time in years, she felt alive again.

Chapter Three

As they entered the coffee shop, Kevin realized that there was something about this skittish girl that he found charming. He could think of no other word to describe it. Missy Schuler was feminine, girlish. She dressed simply, and that appealed to him. She looked so pretty in her jeans and purple sweater. It was a nice change from the usual black outfits a lot of the woman he went out with wore. And her brown hair looked shiny and well cared for. It did more to adorn her than diamonds ever could.

Yes, Missy Schuler appealed to him. She seemed wholesome and nice. He liked how she was quiet and unsure. It made him feel protective toward her. He wanted to take care of her, find out what made her tick.

Of course, her history gave him pause. Once again he was glad he had touched base with Joanne. He wasn't sure what he would do if he ever came face-to-face with her former husband. In his book, guys who were cruel to their wives or girlfriends weren't men at all, just slime. Kevin couldn't imagine someone yelling or constantly berating her, especially a man who had vowed to cherish her before God.

What he did know was that he wanted to see more of her. He wanted to figure out if his feelings were only brotherly, or much more than that. And it sure looked as if she could use a friend. If that was all that was between them, so be it. He had some extra time; he could be that for her.

No matter what, Kevin knew that any type of relationship between them would have to be built gradually. He would have to go slowly with her, let her make the moves. He was afraid that if he came on too strong, he would scare her away.

They sat down at a small table near the front of the shop and ordered two coffees and muffins. Missy looked tense, on edge. He tried to think of the most mundane of conversation topics.

"So, do you have to work today, Missy?"

Missy forced herself to act calm. Just because he was gorgeous and charming was no reason to fall on the floor from the force of a simple question. She forced herself to smile casually. "No, thank goodness.

I'm off tomorrow too. Joanne only opens the museum every other weekend in the winter."

"I guess I should have known that, as much as Joanne has talked about her schedule." He paused. "I usually put in my extra hours in the evenings, so I enjoy my weekends a lot."

"That's nice." She wondered what he would say if she told him that she wanted to see him again. Probably nothing. But, if she didn't tell him, things would be no different than they were at the present time. Lonely.

She spoke again. "So, do you have a lot of plans for next weekend?"

He looked surprised by her question. She shifted uncomfortably. Did she sound too forward? "I mean, I know that most of your family is here. Do you usually get together with them?"

"Depends on everybody's schedule. Actually, I went over to my parents' house this morning."

"So." she smiled impishly. "You . . . you didn't sleep in either."

He flashed her a smile, his teeth white and even. "I'll be okay."

She might as well get this over with. Missy took a deep breath. "Um, I guess you spend a lot of time with your girlfriend too."

He smiled, but his eyes were serious as they met hers. "I would, if I had one."

"You're not dating anybody?" She bit her lip and frowned. Honestly, she sounded like an interrogator!

"Not at the moment. Are you?"

"Gosh, no."

"What?"

"I mean, after Scott . . . I'm not ready for another relationship like that."

"Oh."

Missy closed her eyes. Things were not going well. "That didn't sound right. I'm sorry, I'm trying to ask you something, but I'm just so nervous."

He took a sip of coffee, as if he had all the time in the world to sit in the coffee shop with her. Finally he said, "It's best if you just get it over with."

"Well, I was wondering if you would like to come over to dinner on Friday night? As a thank-you for your help."

"You don't need to do that. It was my pleasure; I would have done it for anyone."

Her heart skipped a beat. Was she just *anyone?* Was she making too much of his benevolence? But she had gone too far to take back her offer. Biting her lip, she forged ahead. "For you, it was a kindness. But to me, your kindness was a godsend."

"I've always thought that good deeds have a way of coming around to others," Kevin replied with a small shrug. "One day it will be your turn to help someone in trouble."

"Fair enough. But until then, dinner seems like the least I can do."

"Then I accept. Thank you."

She smiled in relief. "You're welcome."

They sipped coffee for a few minutes more, then parted ways, both claiming a day of running errands. Missy strolled back to her car, her mind full of plans. Kevin Reece would be her first guest since she had moved into her place, and although she couldn't decorate her house for the occasion like a picture from *Better Homes and Gardens* magazine, she could certainly plan a nice dinner.

Cooking had always been her secret joy, and being able to plan a dinner for a guest gave her a feeling of satisfaction. Even though he wouldn't be coming over for a few days, she went to the library, checked out some of the latest cookbooks, and spent the afternoon perusing recipes and menus.

She finally decided on chicken piccata with fresh linguine, a garden salad, French bread, and a cheesecake for dessert. Each dish was relatively simple and would allow her to prepare some of it in advance.

As she wrote out her list, it was impossible not to compare Kevin with Scott. Kevin was someone who was quietly confident and secure. He carried his good looks unself-consciously and looked strong but not foreboding.

In contrast, Scott had always tried too hard, second-guessing his appearance, planning to work out more, to one day have a better closet of clothes. It didn't seem like those kinds of things had ever crossed Kevin's mind.

And Scott had always tried to prove his masculinity, never doing anything that might harm his "manly" reputation. He had never helped her with household chores, or even gone to the grocery store. Or opened doors for her, or helped her carry her bags. . . .

Absently, she rubbed the scar on her right arm. The two-inch mark served as a symbol of the scars that she carried on the inside. Again, she compared the two men.

Kevin Reece was successful, and a hard worker. He apparently had a promising career in front of him as well. In contrast, Scott had been none of those things. When they had first married, she had been foolish enough to believe that he could have been. He had boasted of grand dreams, then blamed his lack of effort on dozens of excuses. And somehow, it had been her responsibility to take care of the mundane things, like holding down a steady job, paying the bills, cooking dinner, cleaning the house—doing everything exactly right. And, as she remembered, nothing ever had been exactly right to him. He had constantly berated her for being lazy, for not looking nicer, for not doing something exactly the way he had wanted it done.

Missy rubbed another puckered spot of skin on her calf. She should almost thank him for instigating their argument that evening. When she had turned from him in disgust, then tripped over the grill, it had finally, literally, knocked some sense into her. She had realized that she could either look forward to a lifetime of disappointment and pain, or have the freedom to do what she wanted, to make her own choices.

And she had chosen freedom.

Those first months had been tough; she had been so insecure. It had been hard, learning to trust her instincts and to stand up to Scott during their divorce. But she had done it. She had been able to move on with her life and begin again.

Missy looked around her kitchen. Light streamed in through the sheer curtains that hung across the window over the sink. She felt a sense of accomplishment and pride, and it felt good. Yes, the building was old and the furniture shabby, but it was hers. Yes, she worked hard, but now she could have the satisfaction of saving for her own dreams, not just Scott's. And although she was about to be cooking dinner for a man again, this time *she* was the one in charge of the menu. She also knew instinctively that Kevin would not criticize the meal simply out of spite.

She picked up her pencil again to make a few more notes for her meal-in-progress. She could do this. She could plan a wonderful meal for a friend that she was proud of. Things were definitely better now. And she planned to make sure that they stayed that way.

Chapter Four

On Monday morning, Missy almost dropped the file she was holding as she listened to her boss. "Oh, Joanne . . . I don't know."

"You don't know? What is there to think about?" Joanne chuckled. "I think it sounds terrific! Having a Civil War costume party on the third floor of the Memorial Building is just what Payton needs to rejuvenate some interest in the proposed measure."

"But. . . ."

"People will really get a kick out of being in the same place where their ancestors once were," Joanne continued, her voice warm with excitement.

Missy placed her file carefully on the table before speaking. Somehow she had to get Joanne to see that she would be completely in over her head if she tried to take on a job like that. "I think that your idea has merit, and, having a dance in the old building sounds great," Missy agreed slowly, "it's just that I don't think that *I* should be the one in charge of it."

"Why not?"

Missy swallowed hard. "I don't have any experience planning parties or anything."

Joanne smiled kindly. "That's no problem. I know plenty of people who would be more than happy to help you there. I'll give you a list of people to call. My mother would be at the top."

"But . . . wouldn't you be better suited for the planning?"

"I don't have the time. You know I've got those meetings, and Stratton has been working like crazy. Then, the Underground Railroad museum is about to get really busy too. And if I actually had to serve on a committee with my mother, well, we both know what a disaster that would be!" Joanne paused in her explanation and looked at Missy more thoughtfully. "What's the matter?"

"I'm just afraid that I'll do something wrong, that's all. That it won't be how you want it to be."

"If you do something wrong, then we'll fix it together. And I don't know *how* I want it to be, Miss. I just think that holding a dance in the Memorial Building sounds like a good idea." Her voice softened. "Please? I want you to do this for me. I need your help." Joanne pursed her lips together. "I could pay you overtime," she added, brightening at the words.

Missy shook her head in wonder. How could she refuse that? Now there was nothing else to say. Joanne was right; it was a good idea. And no matter how much they might like each other, Joanne was her boss, and taking on tasks like this was part of Missy's job. "All right, I'll do my best," she said cautiously.

"That's all you can do," Joanne answered, then turned back to the papers on the front counter, as if trying to put them in some semblance of order.

Missy watched her with a small smile. It was no secret that paperwork, organization, and deadlines were not Joanne's forte. Not that Joanne couldn't accomplish each task well, it was just that it didn't come naturally. She was brilliant, but a mess. It could take Joanne over an hour just to find a research paper she had written in half that time. With that in mind, it did make sense that Joanne would balk at the idea of planning a dinner/dance in one month's time.

Missy turned back to her filing. Now that the decision had been made, she found herself already forming plans, and she was eager to go to the building and check it out. The Memorial Building had been the only three-story building in Payton during the Civil War and had kept that honor until 1893, for that matter. It was a little run-down, but thanks to a grant that Joanne had written, it had recently been treated to a face-lift on the outside. However, Joanne said the inside of the third floor was a different matter. It needed a face-lift, and fast.

There were invitations to design, and people to call. Missy's head began to spin. She was just about to go to her desk when Joanne spoke again. "By the way, I talked to Kevin a couple of times this weekend."

Missy forced herself to look at Joanne. "Really?"

Joanne nodded. "He told me about your car trouble, and how he picked you up. . . ." Her voice drifted off.

"I'm really thankful that he stopped for me."

Joanne's expression softened. "Thank goodness he did." She paused for a moment and straightened a pile of papers on the counter. "He also said he had coffee with you . . . and that you're going to have him over for dinner."

Heat crept up Missy's neck. "I hope you don't mind."

Joanne looked surprised. "Why would I mind? I think it's terrific that the two of you are forming a friendship."

"I don't think you understand . . . the dinner is just a thank-you," Missy said quickly. "Since he practically saved my life the other night, inviting him for dinner is the least I could do." Already reasons why Joanne wouldn't want her brother to date her were filling her mind. Obviously she would want someone more sophisticated, someone in their circle of friends, to be seeing Kevin. Missy clenched her hand to hide her feelings from Joanne.

"He said he had a good time with you on Sunday." Joanne glanced at her, as if to gauge her reaction. "Not that we were talking about you all that much or anything."

Missy sat down. "Really?"

A smile played around the corners of Joanne's lips as she flipped through her calendar. "Yep. He said you were really sweet and easy to talk to."

"Really?"

Joanne arched an auburn eyebrow in amusement as she nodded. "And he told me all about how your brown hair falls right in the middle of your shoulder blades, as if I didn't know."

Missy gazed blankly into the open file on her lap. "He said that?"

"He did. He also mentioned those blue eyes of yours. . . ."

Missy held up a hand. "Stop. I don't want to hear any more." She laughed.

Joanne chuckled too. "I bet he's going to ask you out soon."

"I doubt that." Missy knew better. Of course she would be thrilled to be asked out by Kevin Reece, but why would he want to date her? He probably had dozens of girls to choose from.

But—what if he did ask her out? Her heart skipped a beat. What would Joanne say if he did? What would Joanne think? Really think? She voiced the words hesitantly. "Would that bother you? If we did go out one day?"

"Why would that bother me?"

"I thought maybe you wouldn't want Kevin to be dating someone like me."

Joanne stared at her, baffled. "Like you how?"

"Well, someone who's divorced, and never went to college, and who's barely scraping by."

"Missy!"

"I'm just trying to say that I imagine you're used to seeing him with a very different type of girl."

"Missy, you are one of the nicest people I've ever met, and you're lovely, to boot."

"Thank you. I just meant that I imagine he's used to someone more sophisticated."

"If by sophisticated, you mean a girl with an attitude, you're right!" Joanne rolled her eyes. "One day I'll tell you about Suzanne. She was a nightmare."

Missy raised her eyebrows. "Suzanne?"

"Never mind her." Joanne took a deep breath, then spoke. "Listen, none of those girls were good for Kevin. Believe me, I'm glad he's seeing you. He needs to make some connections with people, instead of just trying to get his next promotion. He spoke more about you last night than anyone else he's ever dated. I just wanted to let you know."

"Oh, thanks, then."

"No problem."

"Hey, any suggestions for dating your brother?"

Missy hoped the words sounded lighthearted and not desperate.

"Boy, that's tempting." Joanne grinned. "Oh, he'd kill me if I said half the things I'm thinking. No, I'd just say be yourself, and don't get offended if he tries to take care of you a little bit. Kevin's like that—a nurturer. Maybe it's because he's the oldest or something; it comes naturally to him. Just let him help you out. He's truly the most chivalrous guy I know. Perfect manners."

What could she say to that? "All right, I'll keep that in mind," she said, then went to the rear of the building, where her little desk sat. As she seated herself, her thoughts ran in circles through her mind.

Resolutely, she studied her calendar and then began to make plans for the days ahead. She had three classes of fourth-graders arriving in two hours, followed by a meeting with Joanne and the board members to discuss the inventory in the gift shop. But there was still time to begin plans for the party, and to try to visit the old Memorial Building and gather ideas.

She picked up a pencil and began to do just that, giving thanks as always that she was able to concentrate on work and block out any personal problems she might have.

Kevin blinked his eyes and tried once again to concentrate on the stack of papers that lay in front of him. Finally, he gave up and walked to his window. He couldn't get Missy out of his mind. Her smile was so sweet, and her actions so honest. He couldn't remember the last time he had been with a girl and felt that way. Maybe with Susan Phillips during his junior year in high school?

No matter what, spending time with Missy Schuler was much different than any date he had been on lately. There hadn't been any sparring, mild flirtations, or promises, for that matter. Missy hadn't tried to figure out his net worth in two hours of guided conversation. She had just asked him if he'd had a nice day.

And it had been obvious that she was trying to look pretty for him. And she was pretty. Unconsciously, he held out a hand and recalled how silky her hair was, and imagined what it would feel like running through his fingers. He wanted to feel that softness again.

Resolutely Kevin went back to his desk and picked up a pencil. As he began to punch in numbers on his calculator with the eraser, he wondered what she would think if he bought her a rug. Nothing too expensive, just something to curl her toes in at night. Her living room had looked so bare Saturday night. . . . the wooden floor had seemed so cold. She really did need a friend. She needed someone to look out for her a little bit, boost up her confidence, make her feel good. He could do that. Well, for as long as she'd let him, he could.

Chapter Five

Missy put down the phone and stared at it in shock. She had done it; she had not only called Mrs. Reece to ask for advice in planning the party, but she had also made arrangements to meet her and her friend Marianne McKinley at the Memorial Building in a few days. What's more, Mrs. Reece had insisted Missy come to her home that very evening for coffee and dessert, to begin preliminary plans for the dance.

It had been impossible to say no. The woman had been like a cyclone. No, Missy corrected herself, that wasn't fair. Her words hadn't been destructive, just overpowering and overwhelming. She was more like a gale-force wind, leaping from idea to idea. It had been all Missy could do just to hold on tightly. Thank goodness Mrs. Reece had had so many good ideas; it would have been impossible to disagree.

Missy stood up and reluctantly made her way to Joanne's desk. Even though Joanne had told her to call her mother, it still felt strange to make plans with her boss's family without Joanne present.

Joanne glanced up as she approached. "Hey, I meant to thank you earlier for the smooth way you handled that group of rowdy boys," she said.

Missy laughed. "It was no problem. They were just more interested in stories about Indians than in antique kitchen utensils."

"Well, not everybody could have handled them that well. How did you know that story about the pioneer who fended off raiders with a wooden spoon, anyway?"

"Um, I made it up."

Chuckling, Joanne said, "Good for you! That was a great story. How are the plans for the party coming along? I just wrote a note to the town council, encouraging them to promote this fund-raiser. I'll have you look it over later. Stratton thinks sometimes I come off a little pushy where old buildings are concerned."

"I'll be happy to read the letter." Missy paused for a minute, then plunged ahead. "I, ah, called your mother."

A knowing look entered Joanne's eyes. "How did that go?"

"She has got a lot of good ideas."

"My mother's extremely resourceful," Joanne said with a knowing grin. "Do you think that she'll be able to help you out at all?"

"I'll say. Mrs. McKinley is going to meet me at the building later this week to get some ideas."

"She's great. You'll like her."

"But, there's another thing. Your mom invited me to her house for coffee and dessert tonight. To discuss the party."

Joanne burst out laughing. "I bet she's so excited that she can hardly stand it. After all, it's been a good seven months since she had my wedding to worry about. Get ready to be overwhelmed by conversations about balloons, guest lists, and color schemes."

Missy smiled at the image. Joanne certainly seemed to understand what it had been like to speak with her mother about the celebration. But there was more on her mind than just the party. "You don't mind, do you?"

"Mind what?"

"That I'll be at your parents' house . . . I feel like I'm invading your territory."

"Don't be silly. I would never have asked you to call my mom if I didn't want you to, and believe me, getting involved in other people's business is what she does."

"But, I'm working for you . . . and seeing your brother . . . and now visiting with your mom. . . ."

Joanne reached out and gripped Missy's hand. Her eyes grew uncharacteristically serious. "All this family stuff is new to you, isn't it?"

Missy nodded. "I'm so used to only having myself, for better or worse."

Joanne looked as if she were about to blurt something out, then only sighed. "Missy, I come from a big, meddling family. I love them very much. And there's plenty of love there to share with others. It's not going to go away if you receive some of it too. Any of us kids would be the first in line to thank you for redirecting my mother's energies to something besides her kids' lives. Just don't feel obligated to do something you don't feel comfortable with. I have faith that you are the best person to organize this party. I only thought you might appreciate my mother's help."

"Well. . . ."

"No, listen. If you want my mother's help, then go for it! But, if she's driving you crazy, or not listening to your ideas, then I'll help you to politely tell her to leave you alone. And as for Kevin—I'll be honest with you and tell you that I think you guys would make a great couple. But if you only want friendship from him, that's okay too. No matter what, you don't need to worry about your job or your relationship with me."

Shocked that Joanne had guessed her thoughts, Missy hastened to explain herself. "I would never think that you would be that way, Joanne. You've done so much for me."

Joanne tilted her head, studying Missy. "You just don't see it, do you?"

"What?"

"See that I owe you?"

"Of course you don't owe me."

"Missy, don't you recall the first week I started here and you had to show me how to do everything?"

"Well, I was happy. . . ."

"And how I messed up the records, and you had to work an entire weekend without pay to sort them out for me?"

"You just have a problem with organization, that's all."

Joanne sighed. "Missy, I never would have gotten through those first few weeks if it hadn't been for you. I still wouldn't be able to function if not for you. I owe you a lot. Our friendship is not one-sided."

Surprised, Missy realized that Joanne was right. Another layer of uncertainty seemed to melt away. She smiled then, and reached out her arms as Joanne gave her a quick hug.

"There is one thing you ought to do though," Joanne said with a grin.

"What's that?"

"Call up my brother and let him know that you'll be at my mom's house tonight."

"Why?"

"Between my mother and Mrs. McKinley, he'll find out. You might as well be the one to tell him so he doesn't think you're avoiding him."

"But why?" Missy asked again. "Do you think he'll be upset to know I was at your house?"

Joanne's smile broadened at her question. "Oh, no. I don't think he'll be upset at all." Joanne scratched something quickly on a Post-it note. "Here's his number. Go give him a call."

Missy took it and glanced at the clock. Then, seeing that Joanne had several books open on her desk and looked ready to be camped out there for awhile, figured it was time to earn her pay. "Joanne, did you forget about your appointment with the mayor?"

Joanne sat up straight. "Oh, Lord, I did forget! What time is that meeting?"

"In forty minutes."

Abruptly, Joanne stood up, then looked at her cluttered desk in a panic. "Um, do you remember what I promised to have for him?"

Missy picked up the bright blue folder that sat on the corner of Joanne's desk. "You were going to have the action plan ready."

Relief flooded her features. "I did that last night. Thanks, Missy."

"Anytime."

Missy didn't feel quite as sure of herself when she dialed the numbers to Kevin's office two minutes later.

Especially when a sultry female voice answered the phone. "Kevin Reece's office."

"Hello, this is Missy Schuler. Is, uh, Mr. Reece available?"

"One moment, please."

"Missy, is everything all right?" Kevin asked a few seconds later when he came on the line.

"Hi. Joanne thought I should give you a call and let you know that I'll be at your mother's house tonight."

"Really? What's up?"

Assured that he didn't sound like he thought she was invading his space—only curious—she told him about the party and dance, and the conversations she'd had with Joanne.

"I think your mother and her friends are going to be a lot of help when we begin thinking of ways to make it seem like an authentic Civil War dance," she said.

"I bet she already has her sewing machine out and is designing costumes." Kevin chuckled.

"Gosh, I hope so!"

"I bet Mom can hardly wait until you arrive. She loves this stuff."

"I'm sure I'll appreciate her help." Missy paused then; there seemed to be nothing else to say. "Well, I just wanted to let you know."

"Hey, Miss, I was planning to stop by Mom and Dad's tonight, anyway. I'll see you then."

Missy didn't know why, but she blushed at his

words. It almost sounded like he was trying to find a way to see her. "All right. I'll see you later, Kevin. I'm sorry to call you at work."

"Call me anytime, Missy. It's no bother."

Later, she pulled up to the historic building. A small office was kept manned a few hours a week, and after explaining her situation, Missy was given a key to the third floor.

As she made her way up the old stairs, the wood creaked under her weight, and a few clouds of dust filled the air. She gripped the banister harder, and tried to look at the walls objectively. Faded rose chintz, the wallpaper was probably once vibrant and colorful, but now bubbled and peeled at the edges. The dark woodwork was scarred, but in surprisingly good condition. And, although the staircase was narrow, it was manageable.

Finally she arrived at the top of the stairs. After she unlocked the door, she stood in awe of the space that she had been coerced into sprucing up and filling with two hundred people in one month's time. With a sharp intake of breath, she tried again to view the expanse with detachment.

About a dozen pieces of old furniture lay scattered throughout the huge room, each piece covered with moth-eaten, dingy-colored sheets. The woodwork was dull and covered with dust, and the six light fixtures looked to be composed mainly of spiderwebs and broken glass.

An alcove framed the back of the room. An industrial sink, oven, and avocado-colored refrigerator stood sentry. The counters that surrounded the appliances were warped and stained. Missy made a mental note to check into the price of building a partition or wall for the area.

The floor was covered in a dirty gold carpet that someone must have thought attractive in the fifties or sixties. How was she ever going to transform this place into a ballroom? Into a place where hundreds of people would want to spend their time in and get excited about?

Walking in further, Missy took note of the ornate woodwork, the high ceilings, and the charming etched glass. The niche under the windows would look lovely with just a few plants to brighten it up. And all the woodwork needed was some fresh paint. The floorboards would look nice painted white—so fresh and clean.

Her mind began to spin. The room would look lovely in shades of reds, reminiscent of the once opulent decor to which the history books on the building had made reference. And she would tell the men who pulled up the carpet not to stain the wood, just refinish it. The light, natural color would accent the deep shades of the walls nicely.

She continued planning. Wasn't a sale going on at

Madison Fabrics? The curtains would be lovely gold, to accent the bronze light fixtures. And if there was time, matching runners could be made for the buffet tables.

Paintings by local artists and Civil War memorabilia could decorate the walls. Fresh flowers could adorn each table. And everyone could wear costumes.

A smile slowly spread across her lips. Yes, refurbishing the room and preparing for the dance would be a lot of work, but it would be worth it. And she could do it. She was *capable* of transforming this place into something to be proud of.

Joy bubbled through her. She giggled at the feeling. Then, because no one could see her, she twirled in a circle and let out a small cheer.

Chapter Six

After what she had heard from Joanne and Kevin, Missy didn't know why she was surprised to feel so at home in Daphne's house.

The large, sprawling ranch was decorated more beautifully than any house Missy had ever been in before, and the tea service that Daphne used was straight out of a home catalog. At first she felt awkward in such surroundings—after all, these were things she had only seen in magazines—but she soon found out that none of the fancy furnishings took away from the warmth of the older lady's personality. They seemed only to add to her character, the way a good accessory complements a new outfit.

Daphne Reece was beautiful and petite and talked a mile a minute. She also seemed to glide naturally in high heels. Her faded blond coiffure remained effortlessly in place, and her French manicure looked freshly applied. But, it looked as if she had several things in common with Missy too.

She had a number of carefully color-coded files and address books, and she seemed to thrive on organization. She also loved lemon bars and sour cream pound cake, if the dessert she offered tonight was any indication of her tastes.

After a few tense minutes, Missy found herself eagerly conversing with Daphne. She told her about the successful visit to the old office building, and discussed the logistics of scheduling needed repairs. Before long, Missy was copiously writing notes in her yellow notepad and volunteering ideas about flower arrangements and the design of the invitations.

Daphne looked at her in frank appreciation, and even went so far as to brag about her efforts to Mr. Reece. Mr. Reece said little, only patted Daphne's shoulder when she finished describing their tasks.

Taking a break, Daphne served hot tea and cake.

"This is wonderful, Daphne," Missy said in appreciation as she sipped English Breakfast tea from a delicate china teacup.

"Thank you. I hear from Joanne that you like to bake too."

"Well, I like to do that; I just don't have the opportunity very often." She was about to add more when she heard the kitchen door open and Kevin's unmistakable voice carry through.

Daphne sat up, puzzled. "My goodness, that's Kevin. I wonder why he's here."

Missy sought to explain. "I called him, Daphne. Joanne suggested I should."

"Oh, really?"

She nodded. "Joanne thought Kevin might want to know I was over here for some reason. But it didn't matter, he said he was planning to stop by anyway."

Daphne rested her gaze on Missy for a long moment, then let out a girlish giggle. "Gosh, you're right. Jim and I had made plans to visit with Kevin, and in the excitement of planning the party, I had forgotten all about it." She turned as Kevin wandered in. "Hi, dear, I was just wondering when you would show up."

Kevin smiled as he bent down to kiss his mother on her cheek. "I'm sorry, I got caught up with work." As he straightened, he focused his clear gray eyes on Missy. "Hello, Missy. How's it going?"

Missy's breath caught in her throat. He looked so handsome in his navy pinstriped suit, crisp white button-down, and red tie. His blond hair was slightly rumpled, as if he had just run his fingers through it. And, even from her spot a few feet away, she could see the faint shadow of a day's growth of beard across his cheeks. Then, realizing that she needed to answer him, she spoke hurriedly. "Things have been going well. Your mother's a whiz at party planning."

He laughed. "Tell me about it."

"Now, Kevin," Daphne interjected, "We've been having a nice time together."

"We just finished up, and your mother was kind enough to offer some dessert," Missy explained. "I had better be on my way. I don't want to keep you from your time together."

"Don't leave yet," both Kevin and his mom said together. Daphne's cheeks flushed.

"Please stay, dear," Daphne said again, her gaze flickering from Kevin to Missy.

"Well, all right, if you're sure?"

"Positive," Kevin answered with a smile. "How was your day?"

"Busy." Missy laughed, then launched into the story about the rambunctious fourth-graders. She couldn't believe how easy they were to talk to. Mr. Reece joined them shortly afterward, and after an initial worry about his reserved demeanor, Missy began to feel comfortable with him as well.

For their part, the elder Reeces entertained Missy with stories about Kevin when he was younger, and then the escapades all five kids had had together.

One story, in particular, warmed Missy's heart, about when the family had been skiing. Kevin had stayed next to five-year-old Jeremy and taught him to ski when everybody else had just wanted to send him to ski school.

"Poor Jeremy, just didn't want to go to that ski

school," Daphne said. "He couldn't stand to be left out of any of the fun."

"And Cameron had had enough of Jeremy, because he had to share a bed with him," Jim added.

"I got my own because I was the oldest." Kevin laughed.

"Jeremy cried and cried. Finally Kevin couldn't take it."

"It wasn't so bad. He caught on pretty fast."

"You stayed with him on that bunny hill for hours," Daphne said.

"Now, he's the best skier in the family," Jim boasted.

"I'd probably have to hang out on that bunny hill now," Kevin teased.

"I hope he knows how lucky he was to have you," Missy said softly.

"It was no big deal," Kevin said.

"I'm sure it was to him," Missy corrected. For a moment, their eyes met, and Missy felt that same understanding pass between them that she had felt earlier. Her pulse quickened.

Mr. and Mrs. Reece exchanged glances. Jim coughed. "Daphne, I can't get the darn bagel contraption to work. Come give me a hand."

Before she knew it, Missy was alone with Kevin. He stood up and moved to the spot his mother had vacated next to her on the couch. "It's great that you're here. I was going to give you a call tonight."

Pleasure fluttered through her. "You were?"

"Yep. Just to make sure that we were still on for Friday night."

"Oh, I'm planning on it," she said hurriedly, then cursed her awkwardness again. When was she ever going to sound more sophisticated?

They sat for a moment in silence, then Missy became uncomfortably aware that she had been at the Reece's home for over two hours. "I better get on home," she said, standing up. "It's been a long day."

Kevin stood up also. "All right."

On their way out, Kevin led her to the kitchen to say goodbye to his parents. Daphne vowed to give Missy a call within the next few days with more ideas for the party. Then he walked her to the door. "I'm glad you stopped by," he said, lifting her coat from the peg near the door and holding it for her.

"I am too," she replied, then tried to look as if she was used to having men do favors for her as she slid her arms into the sleeves of her jacket. Honestly, she couldn't remember ever having a man hold her coat for her before.

She turned to him to say good-bye, but he only shook his head. "I'll walk you to your car."

Taking her elbow, he guided her down the sidewalk, took her keys from her, and within minutes had not only unlocked her car door, but had turned on the ignition to warm up the heater and engine. It was all done so effortlessly, without fuss, as if he wouldn't have been Kevin Reece if he hadn't done those things.

But Missy noticed every action and appreciated the attention. She wondered if the other girls he had dated had felt the same way, or if they were so used to his good manners that they had simply come to expect them. She hoped that she would never get to that point. It was wonderful to look forward to being pampered.

It was finally time to tell him good night. "I'll call you tomorrow, Miss."

"All right."

He reached out, and gently cupped her neck beneath her hair. "May I kiss you?"

"Oh yes," she said, then closed her eyes as she realized how childish she must sound to him.

But he didn't say anything, his lips just curved upward before they softly met hers, feather light. It was a touch that invited more. Missy sighed and leaned toward him, raising her hands to grip his arms. And she felt pleasure when their lips met again, this time more slowly, as if he were also savoring their contact.

"Good night, Miss," he murmured as he stepped away. "Be careful going home."

"Thank you, I will," she said, then finally slid into her car, reveling in the unaccustomed feeling of sitting in a warm car right away.

Kevin watched her drive away and then sauntered back inside his parents' house. He only had a few minutes before he also needed to get on home. There was a report that he wanted to look over before his conference call at eight, and probably a hundred e-mails awaiting his attention.

He was abruptly halted by the appearance of his parents in the front entryway. He groaned as his mother eyed him with interest.

"Kevin, what was it that you wanted to speak with us about? We hadn't planned to see you tonight."

His dad chuckled. "Or were you more interested in a certain lovely young lady, Kevin?"

It was time to get out of there, fast. "Gee, Dad, I really better get going. . . ."

"I'm sure you will need to, dear, as soon as you sit down with us in the kitchen. Come, have a lemon bar."

Kevin groaned. His mother knew he hated lemon bars. But he did the only thing he ever thought to do with his parents: he obeyed. "All right, I'll be right there," he said slowly, shrugging out of his coat, ready to be interrogated.

His parents had already dug into several bars before he made it to the kitchen. After declining one, as well as the offer of coffee, Kevin sat down at the table with trepidation. He didn't really mind talking about Missy—it was just that his parents had the habit of making him tell them more than he ever originally intended. They would have made excellent interrogators in World War II.

"So, tell us all about you and Missy," his dad said without preamble.

He squirmed and took a deep breath. It was not a good sign that he already felt uncomfortable. "There's not much to say right now, Dad."

"But there might be one day?" Daphne prodded.

"I don't know about our future, Mom."

Her eyes brightened. "But, you are definitely planning a future together?"

His palms began to sweat. "You know that is not what I meant." He coughed, looked around for water. "Besides, I don't really think my relationship with Missy is any of your business." He walked to the cupboard to claim a glass.

Far from being miffed at his words, Daphne shared a look with her husband. "So, your relationship is *private?*"

"Mom, I'm just trying to do something nice for her. Be a friend. She needs a few."

"There's no denying that, son," Jim said. "But, you have to admit that she's an improvement over Suzanne Campbell."

Daphne folded her arms across her chest. "Anyone would be, dear."

Kevin scowled. "Why are you bringing her up?"

"Well, she was the last girl you brought home," Jim said.

"She wasn't so bad."

"She showed up for Easter brunch with a healthy buzz and a major attitude," his mom pointed out.

Kevin closed his eyes. "Haven't we gone over this enough? I've said sorry a hundred times."

His mother narrowed her eyes. "She flirted with Jeremy."

Kevin rolled his eyes at that. "We all know that that was the *least* offensive thing she did. Jeremy loved it." He reached for his glass of water and took a fortifying sip. "Suzanne's history now. Honestly, all I do anymore is work."

Jim nodded. "And that's your problem."

Kevin gritted his teeth in frustration. This was yet another conversation with his parents that he knew he couldn't win. "I thought you were glad I got that promotion."

"I am glad. Proud of you too," his dad answered. "But that doesn't mean I don't think you're working too hard. You need to enjoy yourself, come home some nights when there's still daylight."

"Like tonight," Daphne said.

Kevin studied his parents, seated side by side across the table from him—so content with each other, so relaxed in their relationship. Were relationships like that still possible? With the wisdom of his twenty-seven years, he knew that they weren't going to give up their questioning unless he gave them reason to. "I'll think about what you said," he murmured. "But

I need to get on home. I've got a meeting to get ready for."

Daphne glanced at her husband, then nodded her head. "Well, all right, dear. Be careful driving home."

"I will."

Within minutes he had shrugged on his coat and was back in his Lexus. There was little traffic; he knew he'd be in his own home in no time. But he still felt the emptiness that he had been afraid to admit to his parents. It was getting harder and harder to know he was going home to an empty house.

Making a sudden decision, he picked up his cell phone, and at a stoplight, located Missy's number and punched it in. After two rings, she answered. "You make it home all right?" he asked.

"Yes," she replied, then spoke again. "Is everything okay?"

He smiled into the receiver. He didn't really know. "Yep, I was just driving home and thought of you."

"Oh. Well, um, I hope your meeting goes all right tomorrow."

"Thanks." He stopped at another light, and gazed at the empty streets, and the lights in the windows of the two houses to his left. "It's just another meeting," he stated, then frowned. His words startled him. For the first time, he wasn't ready to lose sleep over the outcome of every hour at work. "Hey, I didn't wake you, did I?"

"No, I was just sitting in bed, reading."

She sounded warm and cozy. Longing to be that way hit him hard. "Good. Well, I'll see you Friday."

"All right. Sleep well, Kevin."

Her words brought him unfamiliar warmth. When was the last time anyone had said those words to him? "Thanks, Missy. Good night."

He shut his phone off just as he pulled into his garage. And as he pulled his briefcase out and opened it on the kitchen table, for the first time in years, he realized he was actually looking forward to the weekend.

Chapter Seven

It was 7:00 on Friday, and he hadn't arrived yet. Once more, Missy scanned the living room and kitchen. Everything was in its place. She had put an old white sheet over her table and colorful napkins over it to liven it up. The table was already set, and ivory tapers were waiting to be lit. Even though the dishes were old, she thought the table was set as nicely as could be.

The wooden floor had been swept, her furniture dusted. Wonderful smells wafted in from the kitchen. All she had left to do was boil the noodles, and then toss them in the lemon-garlic sauce she had already prepared.

She had even gone out to the mall and found a new outfit that had been marked down 70 percent because of a tear in the skirt. She had been able to mend it in minutes and was now sporting the outfit, the pink blouse bringing a bloom to her cheeks. Missy knew the outfit wouldn't hold a candle to the designer clothes that Kevin's usual acquaintances probably wore, but she did think that she looked nice.

It was then that all of her old insecurities resurfaced. What was she thinking? This wasn't a date to Kevin Reece; this was another opportunity for him to be chivalrous. Of course he wasn't going to say no to someone's meager attempt to say thank you.

Just then his car pulled up. Missy held a hand to her stomach to calm the sudden attack of nerves, then took a deep breath as she waited for him to climb the four stairs that led up to her door. As soon as the doorbell rang, she pasted a relaxed smile on her face and opened the door.

And there he stood, actually holding a bouquet of flowers, the kind that she had seen next to the check-out stand for seven dollars. "Hello," she said, "please come in."

"Hi, Missy." His eyes were warm as he stepped in. "These are for you."

She took the bouquet and inhaled its fragrance with pleasure. "Thank you, that was so thoughtful."

He shrugged. "It was nothing."

The bouquet looked and smelled heavenly, but it paled in comparison to Kevin Reece. He was dressed in khakis, a worn chambray shirt, and the same barn jacket that she had seen when they'd had coffee together. His blond hair was damp; he had obviously showered right before he came over. He smelled like woodsy cologne and soap.

Suddenly she remembered her manners. "Won't you come back to the kitchen? I was just about to boil the noodles."

He shrugged off his jacket, hung it on the end of the banister, and then followed her down to the small kitchen.

A salad was waiting on a counter, as well as a pitcher of iced tea. "Would you like some tea?"

"That would be great, thanks."

She was just about to prepare a glass for him when he reached out and brushed her forearm. "I can do this. Let me help you."

"All right," she said, trying not to convey how much even his simple touch affected her. But she couldn't help it; Kevin's presence seemed to fill up her whole kitchen. It was all she could do to focus on anything else. "I'll, ah, cook the pasta."

A fleeting smile crossed his lips. "Okay."

After Kevin poured two glasses, he leaned against the counter and watched her make last-minute preparations. "My mom has a favorite story about making dinner for my dad when they were dating. Would you like to hear it?"

Anything to calm her nerves. "Sure."

With that, he began to talk, his voice low and relaxed, telling a few tales about his parents, and then another about growing up in a house with five kids. She found herself captivated by the stories, and was content to just listen and laugh as she drained the pasta, added cheese and butter, and then took the chicken out from the oven. Soon they were sitting across from each other and digging in to the meal.

"This is wonderful, Missy," Kevin said after taking a few bites.

"Thank you. I was hoping that you would like it."

"Do you cook a lot?"

"Not really. I've been so busy, and it's never the same to cook just for one."

A smile played at the corners of his mouth. "I know how that is, nothing is ever the same by yourself. It's hard." He paused for a moment. "Are you used to living alone after your marriage?"

She unconsciously rubbed the scar on her arm under the pink fabric. "It's probably no secret that my marriage wasn't good, Kevin. I should never have married Scott—I think I realized that in less than a week. I kept trying to make it work. But in the end, nothing ever made it better." She stopped, realizing that she had been droning on about things Kevin hadn't even asked about.

"But to answer your question, yes—I'm used to it. Gosh, I think it's been almost four years now. Actually, I like living on my own, especially now that I live here. Before, I was in a studio apartment and there wasn't much room at all."

"I'm sorry you've had to go through so much," he said, his expression tender.

She bit her lip to keep from tearing up. "Me too," she murmured. So very few people had said that. Most just pretended that she had never been in a difficult marriage, that she didn't struggle every day to steer her life in a different direction.

They ate in silence for the next few minutes, and then after clearing the dishes, Kevin sat on the lone couch in the living room. Missy occupied herself by slicing the cheesecake onto plates and brewing coffee.

"Thanks again for having me over," he said as she joined him, the dessert on a small tray. "It was very good, but, like I told you, unnecessary."

"It was nothing." Missy handed him a plate. "Do you have to go in early for work tomorrow?"

"Yeah, but that's okay."

"But on a Saturday. . . ."

"It should only be for a few hours." He shrugged. "Actually, I've tried recently to make a concerted effort to stay away from the office."

"And is it working?"

He chuckled. "Hey, I'm here, aren't I?"

Her eyes widened at the implication. Realizing that the reason he had to go in on Saturday was because he was at her house instead of at work made her want to apologize. "I. . . ."

He deftly cut her off, as if he knew yet another apology was on the way. “So, where did you learn to cook?”

She smiled at the question. “My mom.”

“Was she a good cook?”

“Yes, but not the gourmet kind or anything. She could follow a recipe well. She taught me to do that also.”

“Like tonight?”

Missy chuckled. “Yep, just like tonight.” She leaned back, surprised at the memories that surfaced from so long ago. “Sometimes she and I would see a menu in a magazine and make the whole thing, every dish. Usually there would enough food for the whole street!”

Kevin leaned back on the couch, obviously enjoying her story. “You’d have some leftovers, huh?”

“Leftovers for a week!” She laughed. “But it was worth it. We’d spend the whole day in the kitchen. She taught me the value of planning out meals and organization.”

“Does she live nearby?”

“Oh, no. When I got married, she moved to Florida in one of those snowbird communities.” She shrugged, wondering when the distance between her and her mother had turned into so much more than just miles. “We’ve drifted apart ever since.”

Kevin looked surprised by her admission. Missy

reached out to touch his arm, to emphasize her words. "Not everyone has a family like yours, Kevin."

His eyes softened, and he placed his hand over hers. "I know, it's just too bad. . . ."

"No, it's all right." She corrected him. "I accepted our relationship a long time ago." Missy took a deep breath and forced her lips to form an easy smile. "Are you ready for dessert?"

"Of course."

She poured the coffee and then spent the next thirty minutes chatting about desserts, work, and Payton. Even though they hadn't run in the same circles, both were pleased to realize that they knew many of the same people. They laughed about one of the checkout ladies at the grocery store as well as the constant state of road construction in their small town.

Before Missy knew it, dessert was finished and Kevin was looking regretfully at his watch. "I hate to say it, but I've got to go," he said, standing up.

She did the same and walked him to the door. "Thank you for coming over, and for the flowers, and for, well, everything."

"You're welcome." He picked up his jacket and easily slipped it on. "I had a nice time tonight, Missy."

Her heart quickened. "Me too."

"I'd like to take you out next Friday night."

"Why?" The word spilled out before she could help herself.

He laughed. "Do I have to have a reason?" he teased. "How about because I'd like to see you again?"

Honestly, where were her manners? She swallowed hard. "Saturday night sounds wonderful. Thank you."

He stepped toward the door, then immediately turned back to her. His hand reached out towards her, then dropped to his side. "Before, with other girls, things just always kind of happened." He paused, and Missy noticed a flush appear on his cheeks. "But I don't want to scare you, or do something you don't want."

Missy stepped closer. "What?"

He raised his hand again. This time it came in contact with her shoulder, skimming the ends of her hair. "Missy, may I kiss you good night again?"

She was sure her mouth was hanging open. She couldn't remember anyone ever asking for permission before. All she could manage was a slight nod.

Then she felt, rather than saw, Kevin step closer, carefully raise his fingers to the nape of her neck, and lightly brush his lips against hers. His lips felt cool and dry, just like they had the other night. He lifted his head a fraction, met her gaze, and then kissed her again, this time pressing more firmly against her lips, slowly covering her mouth. She raised her hands to finally give into temptation and run her fingers through his hair.

A tremor raced through her. The beginnings of his beard felt scratchy against her cheek, and his hands felt so warm as they traced a pattern along her spine. She sighed. Never had she known that a kiss so chaste could trigger so many feelings.

She tilted her head slightly to meet his gaze.

"That was nice," he said, his eyes smiling. "I could get used to this."

Pleasure filled her.

His hand brushed a stray strand of hair away from her cheek. "I'll call you this week."

"All right."

He opened the door. A burst of cool air rushed in. "Good night. Don't forget to lock up."

"I won't. Good night."

Missy watched him walk down the steps toward his car, then shut the door and locked it tightly before heading to the kitchen to tackle the stack of dishes.

As she filled the sink with soapy water and began to scrape the plates, she thought again about the dinner, the conversations, and of course, Kevin's kiss. For the first time in her life, someone decent had taken an interest in her, someone who she wanted to see again.

She even had a date with him next week. She felt happy, and pleased, her mood buoyant and optimistic. It was a good feeling, one that she wanted to savor.

Chapter Eight

By the following Friday, Missy found herself practically living on the third floor of the Memorial Building. Between scrubbing and painting walls and coordinating repairmen, she had kept plenty busy. In addition, there were calls to be made about invitations and guest lists, not to mention her other responsibilities at the museum. Each night she went home exhausted, knowing that she was accomplishing a huge feat.

This day she had a lot of company, and to say things were not going well was a bit of an understatement. Daphne and Marianne McKinley, along with quite a few ladies from the historical society board, were all assembled on the third floor of the Memorial Building, and no one was happy about it.

It was in direct contrast to the last meeting Missy had had with them a few days before. At that meeting, both ladies had been agreeable and easygoing. But now, in a swift personality shift, they seemed to have taken charge and were giving orders. Of course, it was up to her to keep them in line—but that was far easier said than done.

Missy sighed as she recalled how Joanne had 'managed' to have a prior commitment and had sent Missy into battle alone. She felt a lot like a sacrificial lamb, waiting to be slaughtered by the women. They had grand plans in mind for this dance, and both they and she knew that Missy Schuler was out of her league.

For her part, she could readily admit that she had no experience in throwing society galas, decorating Civil War landmarks, or telling rich ladies what to do. And to make matters worse, a few of those women looked as if they were counting on that fact in order to steamroll their ideas right on through.

Aggravated, Missy scanned the copious notes she had taken just the night before. She had even naively devised a tentative timetable and task sheet. But so far, all she had been able to do was stand out of the ladies' line of fire. One woman had even brought along a measuring tape and was talking about hiring a decorator to sew some curtains in a lovely sage green. Sage green? Against the blood-red walls? And how were they going to be able to afford that anyway?

Missy didn't think her budget included draperies like those.

She was just about to tell them that when the door opened and a young woman about her age came in, dressed in maternity clothes, her large belly leading the way. Missy watched her scan the room, narrow her eyes when she saw what the women were doing, and then finally approach them.

"Hi, Missy? I'm Mary Beth Reece," she said with a grin. Seeing Missy's confused expression, she clarified. "I'm married to Cameron, Joanne's brother."

"Nice to meet you. I'm Missy Schuler."

"I've heard a lot about you from Joanne."

"I could say the same about you," Missy said. "Didn't you have that Civil War strongbox in your backyard?"

Mary Beth chuckled. "The one and only."

"I've really enjoyed looking at it, and the papers that you donated to the museum. It's been a big hit."

Mary Beth smiled warmly. "I'm glad." She pointed to the gaggle of ladies. "I see my mother and Daphne over there. Are they trying to take over yet? Joanne called and asked me to stop by after school if I had a chance."

"Kind of like a rescue mission?"

"As you know, Joanne chickened out," Mary Beth said bluntly. "I thought I'd come and give you some support. My mom and Daphne can be a bit of a handful, I admit." She narrowed her eyes as her mother reached into her handbag and pulled out a handful of fabric swatches. "Missy, all I can say is that you should have seen what they were like when we were searching for that strongbox."

"They were excited?"

"Oh my gosh, they were two women on a mission! Plus, I had just bought my place, so they decided I was in need of their decorating sense too. Thank goodness for Cameron."

"Those ladies are very nice." Missy felt honor bound to reply. "They were very gracious when it was just the three of us the other day. But, it's just a little hard dealing with all of these ladies together, all. . . ." She paused for a moment to count. "Ten of them. They know each other so well."

Mary Beth nodded. "It can be overwhelming."

"Yes, it can." Missy glanced at the women again, who were now in a deep discussion about the merits of table decorations made with sweetheart roses and little brass bugles. Oh, Lord. How could she afford fifty bugles?

Mary Beth leaned against the window frame and rested her left palm on her distended stomach. "What you need, Missy, is a plan to channel these women's energies."

Missy held up her notes. "I have that," she said. "I'm just afraid that they don't care right now. I think I'm out of my league."

Mary Beth chuckled. "Believe me, you're not.

Joanne's told me about how great you are at work. And I heard that you're organized too. What these ladies need is a little gentle persuasion." She moved her hands to her hips and shook her head as she overheard two of the women discussing hiring a catering staff. "Would you like me to help you with crowd control?"

They glanced at Daphne. She had pulled up an expanse of carpet and was kneeling on the exposed floor; mindless of the damage it could do to her silk pantsuit.

Missy knew better than to ignore Mary Beth's offer. At this point, she needed all the help she could get. "I'd love the help, if you don't mind."

Mary Beth beamed. "Hey, did I tell you that I teach kindergarten for a living? I have lots of experience ordering people around." She stepped forward. "Mom?"

Mrs. McKinley stopped talking to Daphne when she heard her daughter. "Mary Beth," she said, coming forward. "It's nice to see you. What brings you here?"

"I just happened to be in the neighborhood. Joanne called me at school and asked if I'd stop by to see your progress."

Daphne came forward, also, followed by the rest of the ladies. Instantly Mary Beth was questioned about her pregnancy, baby names, and her health. Missy was impressed with how Mary Beth answered each question patiently, then abruptly changed tacks during a lull in conversation and went for the kill.

"Missy was just telling me about her plans and timetable for this project. You must be so impressed."

The ladies looked taken aback. "Well, actually," Mrs. Reece admitted, "we were fairly preoccupied with some plans of our own."

Missy knew it was time to jump into the conversation. She tried to sound more self-assured than she felt. "I think that's great. I knew it was a good idea to ask for your assistance. But, unfortunately, we have a timetable and a budget to adhere to." She passed out copies of her schedule before the others could say a word.

"But. . . ." a lady in a black sweater set sputtered.

"Goodness," Mary Beth said, when everyone had a copy. "Just look at all the careful forethought that Missy has put into this. I'm certainly impressed."

Missy hid a smile. Mary Beth used the same exact tone that she used when giving museum tours to the six-year-olds. Enthusiastic but firm.

Marianne slipped her glasses onto her nose as she read the documents, then moaned. "This is an awfully small budget."

"Hardly what I had imagined," another lady added, dismayed.

"Perhaps. . . ." A third lady began to speak, but Missy interrupted her.

"As you can see, we need to go ahead and assign jobs today, as well as form the steering committee for this project. I'm so pleased that y'all are so eager to help."

"But I don't see curtains listed," Mrs. Weinberg protested. "Only the cost of fabric."

"You're right. We can't afford to have them made . . . but we could make them ourselves."

Twenty pairs of eyes stared at her in surprise.

Missy coughed. "Remember, ladies, this ball is a fund-raiser. Our object is to make money, not spend it all before it even takes place."

"I realize that, dear," Daphne said delicately, "but I'm not sure if the curtains are the right articles to count pennies on."

Mary Beth interrupted. "Mom, remember when we made curtains for my place? Wasn't that fun?"

Marianne gave her daughter a look that suggested the experience had been anything but. "I do remember that," she said slowly.

"I bet we could make some curtains in no time, for a fraction of the cost."

"But the flowers, the band, the invitations. . . ."

"Did you know the high school band has been practicing hard for competitions? And they even have a performance choir?" Missy looked around at the ladies.

Mrs. Reece looked bemused. "Imagine that."

"I think they would make a great band for this party, perfect for promoting Payton's community spirit." Missy continued.

Mary Beth spoke then. "Boy, imagine the publicity this would create for Payton. Not only did the town's leading ladies sponsor a dance to help raise funds, but they also enlisted the high school's help. I bet all of those band members' parents would buy tickets to come see their kids perform too."

"And the flower arrangements?"

Mary Beth smiled serenely. "Mrs. Hewitt? Remember when you came to my home economics class years ago and showed us how to make our own arrangements?"

"But that was years ago!"

Mary Beth simply folded her arms over her stomach.

Daphne grinned broadly at her daughter-in-law, then turned to face the other women. "I believe that the gauntlet has just been thrown in our direction, ladies. Our task is to create an economical extravaganza, on time, and under budget."

Several women looked shocked. "But, we've never done anything like this. . . ."

"But imagine the thrill," Marianne said, obviously warming to the idea. "Never again would our husbands claim that our fund-raiser dinners cost more to put on than they made."

"We could actually show a real profit!" A lady in a designer suit looked wistful. "Oh, this brings back memories of when I first got married. My Paul and I decorated our whole house for next to nothing. I was so good at garage sales back then."

A few ladies murmured in agreement.

"What a wonderful idea, Missy," Daphne said. "I just knew that Joanne was right about having you take charge of this dance."

Stunned, Missy nodded. "Thank you."

"And how is Kevin?" Daphne asked suavely. "Missy is dating my eldest," she said as an aside to the group.

"He's, ah, fine."

"You two looked so cute together at my house the other night."

Several women exchanged shrewd glances toward each other, and then looked toward Missy. "Thank you," she said again, slightly horrified by the attention.

"And your dinner?" she continued. "I heard you cooked him dinner."

Missy tried to ignore the knowing looks thrown in her direction. "Um, it went well, I think. I made chicken."

Daphne beamed at the tidbit. "Kevin loves chicken."

Missy shifted uncomfortably. *Didn't everyone?*

"Well, let's go ahead and sign up on these volunteer sheets, then," Mrs. Webster said.

"And let's plan an all-day work session in one week," Daphne added. "Would that work for you, Missy?"

Quickly Missy scanned her notes. By then, the carpet should have been pulled and the floors sanded. Looking up, she said, "That should work out just fine. If not, then perhaps we could meet at the museum."

Plans were finalized, and before she knew it, the ladies had gone and all that remained of their group was a list of signatures and the lingering scent of expensive perfume.

Missy looked at Mary Beth in awe. "I don't know how to thank you enough. I never could have done this without you."

Mary Beth patted her on the arm. "I didn't do anything special—I just got their attention. It was your list and timetable that inspired them."

"You think?"

"Well, that and the Payton High School band."

"How so?"

Mary Beth laughed. "You took off the pressure. For once the ladies could put aside their reputations for over-the-top receptions and just concentrate on the goal of the party, which is to raise money and awareness for the historical society. It's an awesome idea, Missy."

"But it was just my ignorance," Missy countered. "It actually didn't occur to me to reserve a string orchestra."

Just then, Joanne joined them. "Is the coast clear?" she asked, looking around as if Daphne and Marianne might suddenly pop out of the floorboards.

"Yes, and no thanks to you, Jo," Mary Beth chided her.

"I'm sorry, but all those women together give me the willies."

"But one of them is your mother!"

Joanne grinned. "Need I say more? Besides, when they join together, those ladies can be positively dangerous."

Both Missy and Mary Beth briefed her on the party preparations and showed her the committees that the ladies had taken charge of.

Joanne surveyed the lists and nodded in agreement. "So, how many days until this shindig?"

"Twenty-two and counting."

Joanne looked at Missy seriously. "Tell me honestly: Can it be done? Can we pull off a Civil War party in that short of time?"

"Yes it can be done," Missy said with more confidence than she felt. "I'll make sure of it."

Joanne sat down on the edge of a covered chair. "Good. Now we can get to the important stuff." She smiled mischievously. "Fill me in on your date with Kevin. How did your dinner turn out?"

"I think it went well."

Mary Beth took a seat next to Joanne and propped her feet up on a stray box. "You 'think it went well'—what kind of answer is that? Tell us all about it."

"I cooked chicken and cheesecake."

Mary Beth chuckled. "I know, I heard you tell my mom that."

"We don't care about the menu." Joanne grinned as she rubbed her hands together. "Tell us the good stuff."

Missy hedged. "I also made a salad?"

Joanne groaned. "Come on. How did you get along?"

Visions of their kiss sprang to mind. "Pretty well."

Mary Beth gazed at her with a bemused expression. "I think Kevin's so cute. He's so capable and dreamy."

"Dreamy?" Missy laughed.

Mary Beth tilted her head to the side. "Kevin is like an ancient liberator; he's just waiting for someone to save."

Joanne laughed. "He's always been like that too. Always responsible, always thinking of duty and what the right thing is. So boring that way."

Boring was the last way she would describe him. "Believe me, after the men in my life, that's a welcome change."

Mary Beth and Joanne shared a look. "I guess so."

Missy shook her head at their looks of pity. "I'm fine. And it could have been worse—Scott wasn't physically abusive—just a jerk. And I got out before it got worse, thank goodness."

Joanne stood up and impulsively engulfed Missy in a hug. "Thank goodness is right."

Chapter Nine

It was already 6:00 by the time the three women locked up the third floor and exited the building. After saying goodbye to Mary Beth, Missy and Joanne walked down the street to where their cars were parallel parked. While the day was fairly sunny for the middle of March, a chill hung in the air, encouraging Missy to pull her jacket closer to her body.

Joanne pointed to a row of young apple trees that a troop of boy scouts had planted the year before in the median of the road. Already each tree was budding. Missy breathed a sigh of relief. She, as much as anyone, was ready to welcome the warmer air and the change of seasons.

They passed a few men exiting the hardware store on their right. Missy said hello while Joanne spoke with them briefly, asking about their families. Once again, Missy was amazed at how many people knew Joanne Sawyer. She had a sunny way about her that drew others like a magnet.

Finally they approached her boss's car. As Missy searched in her tote for her keys, Joanne spoke.

"I can't believe you have gotten so much accomplished! You and my mom make a good team," Joanne said with a trace of envy. "All I ever end up doing with her is getting annoyed because she always thinks of things that I wished I would have."

Missy shrugged. "I can't describe it . . . your mom and I just seem to click. I really like being with her."

"The feeling's mutual. She thinks that you're the best thing that ever happened to me."

Missy smiled at the compliment. "And here I thought Stratton was."

"Well, that goes without saying," Joanne said with a gleam in her eye. "Stratton is just about as perfect a man as a girl could ever hope for."

Missy couldn't contradict Joanne's words. Stratton Sawyer was pretty terrific. He had become the town's doctor the previous year and, once Joanne had taken him under her wing, had settled in easily. Missy had heard dozens of people sing his praises. He had a reputation for being competent as well as having an easygoing, good-natured manner. It didn't hurt that he was gorgeous as well. Missy remembered hearing one lady brag the other day that they had the most handsome doctor in the county. It was a fitting description. Stratton had dark brown hair and clear, piercing blue eyes.

In addition, he appeared to be constantly amused by his wife. He seemed to understand that Joanne needed to flit around from project to project. He also knew that she was far more sensitive than most thought, and encouraged her tender heart. They made a nice couple. And Joanne positively glowed whenever she saw him.

Joanne claimed her keys and jangled them in her hand. "Speaking of good guys," Joanne said with a sly grin, "I hear you've got a date with my brother tonight."

"Well, yes I do." Missy shifted uncomfortably. "We're going to see that new movie, *Evan's Army,* and then to dinner at The Cork. Have you ever been there?"

"Yep. Oh, you're going to love it. Just wait until you try their prime rib. It's just to die for."

"I've never been there," Missy tried to say nonchalantly, although she supposed it would be obvious. She had never had the money to spend on extravagant restaurants. "Um, what do you think I should wear?"

"Let's see. It's not real fancy . . . maybe something kind of casual-elegant. You're going to that dumb war movie first. . . . I'd wear slinky slacks or a long skirt. Maybe something in black."

She didn't have anything like that. In fact, she didn't think the discount store where she had bought her last few things even knew what casual-elegant meant. Missy wasn't sure she did either. She mentally reviewed her checking account, and knew that there was no room for frivolous spending. "Hmm," she said slowly, hoping she didn't sound as bewildered as she felt. "I'll see what I can dig out of my closet."

But something in her expression must have told Joanne that there was more to her response than she let on. "Missy, isn't your house near here?" she asked gently. "How about I stop by and help you pick something out?"

It was tempting. Joanne was creative and usually impeccably dressed. It would be fun to get her advice too. But visions of her worn furniture and threadbare hall carpet came to mind. What would Joanne think, coming from that beautiful house that her parents lived in? "No, that's all right."

Joanne reached out and touched her arm. "Don't worry about having a mess. Stratton's always after me to put my breakfast dishes in the dishwasher . . . but more likely than not, I leave them on the table. Believe me, a mess will just make me feel more at home."

Unfortunately, everything in her spartan house was put away, serving to show just how empty it was. She was just about to tell Joanne no again, but the pull to have a girlfriend to giggle over outfits was too strong. "Thanks, if you're sure you don't mind."

"Great! I'll follow you there."

Within minutes, they had gotten in their cars and

driven the six blocks to Missy's duplex. Although she began to feel the familiar pangs of doubt, Missy forced herself to remember that this place was all hers. She had paid for the down payment and rent all by herself. There was nothing about that to be ashamed of. They parked in front of her door, and then Joanne followed Missy inside.

If Joanne was taken aback by Missy's place, she was too well mannered to show it. After a small pause, Joanne began to talk about Kevin and ways for Missy to do her hair.

Her enthusiasm was catching, and before long, Missy was pulling out clothes from her closet without embarrassment, and laughing at Joanne's comments.

Finally, after encouraging Missy to model different outfits, Joanne pronounced a sky blue sheath the perfect thing. Missy had bought it two years ago for church; it had come with a fancy jacket. But Joanne encouraged her to wear the sleeveless dress alone.

"In March?"

"That's what coats are for, silly," Joanne replied.

Missy still felt doubtful. Did it look like a church dress gone wrong? Would Kevin laugh at her, think she was trying too hard? After all, he probably dated girls all the time who were poster girls for casual elegance. And it showed the scars on her arm too. "I don't know. . . ."

"I know that Kevin loves blue, Missy, and girls in dresses."

"Really?"

"Really." Joanne nodded. "Kevin really has a thing for femininity. I personally think he was born in the wrong era. He would have been the perfect Southern gentleman, complete with standing when a girl entered the room and everything. He loves that stuff."

Missy looked at Joanne and smiled. It was so obvious that Joanne thought her brother was both ridiculous and wonderful at the same time.

"I know Kevin would love you in this. You look nice in blue, and the simple design offsets your pretty features all the more. You ought to leave your hair loose too."

Well, that did it. Missy was out of excuses. If Joanne thought she could get away with this casual-elegance, then she would believe that she could too. "All right, thanks for your help."

But Joanne didn't look in any hurry to leave. She curled up on Missy's couch as if she were ready to chat for an hour. "I know I need to leave and that you've got to get ready . . . but this couch just looked so cozy. Do you mind if I stay another five minutes?"

"Of course not." Missy looked at her friend in appreciation, then joined her on the couch. "Sitting down for a minute sounds great."

"I'm glad we're becoming friends," Joanne said.

"Me too."

"I really admire you, you know."

"Me? Why?"

Joanne tilted her head to the side, her long auburn braid draped over a shoulder. "Here you are, on your own, after a crummy marriage. I had a hard time adjusting when my business burned down, and I had a whole slew of people ready to help."

Joanne probably had no idea how much her comments meant to her. It felt so good to know that she didn't have to face life alone. "It has been hard," she commented, "but I'm okay."

Joanne pursed her lips. "Missy, I know how you got that scar on your arm."

Self-consciously, Missy rubbed the scar. "Scott was a jerk, I'll give him that. And, I'm far better off without him. But I can't blame my accident completely on him," she admitted. "It's not like he pushed me, Joanne. I literally ran into it. We had been fighting, and I turned in a hurry and tripped."

"Well, you're going to be much better off with my brother."

"I'll agree that I'm much better off without Scott," Missy hedged. "But I don't know if Kevin has those kinds of feelings toward me."

"What do you mean?"

"I wonder if he feels more pity or friendship instead of love. . . ."

Joanne crossed her arms over her chest. "You're crazy if you believe that."

Missy sighed. "Joanne—look at me. I was in trouble the first time your brother and I met. And he knows about my past. I'm at such a disadvantage with him, in so many ways."

"How can you say that?"

Missy shook her head. "Well, let's see," she began, counting off the reasons on her fingers. "First of all, I can barely support myself month to month . . . and Kevin has just received a promotion. I haven't even finished community college; he's got a master's in business administration. I don't have any family, and very few friends, he's got a wonderful family, and a large circle of friends." Missy paused, shaken by hearing the contrasts aloud. "I know that he mainly just wants to help me . . . but I don't want him to pity me, Joanne."

Joanne's gaze looked pained. "Missy, I don't think it's that way at all, and I know my brother doesn't. I think he wants to date you, not save you!" She hopped off the couch as she continued. "And I also happen to think that you're selling yourself short. Kevin and I have had a lot of opportunities growing up . . . he would never fault you because of your circumstances."

"I just don't want him to look at me and think 'poor Missy,' or 'look what a mess she's in now' . . . or worse, 'how can I help her get out of this mess.' I want him to want to be with me for me, for what I can give him . . . which maybe isn't much right now."

She stood up. "Thanks so much for helping me pick out an outfit, Joanne. And, thanks so much for listening to me. It helps so much to know that I have a friend like you."

Joanne's gray eyes softened. "You do, you know. I am your friend no matter what."

"I know that," Missy replied softly, then gasped when she glanced at the clock. "Oh my goodness! I've got to go get ready! Your brother will be here in an hour."

Joanne's own eyes widened as she saw the time. "You're right, I've got to get out of here! Stratton's going to be wondering where I am too, if I don't get a move on. I'll call you tomorrow."

"Great, and I'll tell you how our date went."

Joanne slipped on her coat. "Have a good time! Eat some dessert and those yummy little crab cakes for me, okay?"

Missy laughed. "No problem. Good night, Joanne."

Chapter Ten

When Missy opened the door, Kevin stood there in shock. Gone were the jeans and cute sweater sets that he was accustomed to seeing her in. In their place was a lovely blue dress, simple and elegant. In addition, she wore silky nylons, and navy pumps. And she had done something different with her hair too. It was curled, and the shiny tresses hung in waves against her bare shoulders. He loved it down.

Not too many girls had hair that fell past their shoulders . . . and he loved to see it cascade down her back, to imagine sinking his fingers into it and burying his face in its softness.

The blue of her dress brought out the color of her eyes, and she was wearing more makeup than usual. Her lips seemed fuller, her eyes glowed.

In short, Missy Schuler looked absolutely lovely.

Then, realizing he was standing there like an idiot, he handed her a bouquet of tulips. "Here . . . these are for you."

Missy accepted the flowers with a smile, and then stepped back, allowing him entrance. "Thank you. Would you like to come in?"

Nodding, he stepped in and closed the door behind him as she walked to the kitchen to put the tulips in water.

"I can't believe you found these in March! The ones in my window boxes have only just begun to sprout." She fingered the soft petals reverently. "Thanks again for these. I love tulips."

He watched her fill up a water pitcher and cursed himself for not actually bringing the flowers in a vase. Next time. "Um, the florist said that Holland is going to have a bumper crop this year," he said inanely.

Missy looked at him curiously. "I hadn't heard that." She came back into the room and set them on the coffee table. "Well, these are certainly going to brighten up my day tomorrow."

Her eyes met his, and Kevin was irritated to feel his face heating. "You look beautiful, Miss."

Surprise filled her features. "Thank you. Joanne actually came over to help me pick out something to wear."

He didn't know what to think about Joanne being involved in his dates. "Really?"

Missy stood up and did a little twirl. The skirt belled out a little and gave him a better look at her legs. "This dress is described as casual-elegant, for your information."

He laughed at the description. "And here I thought it was just blue. Are you ready?"

She nodded, then led him to her door. Within minutes, they were ensconced in Kevin's Lexus, making their way to the movie theater.

When they were seated by the maître d' three hours later, Missy turned to him and smiled. "This is so nice."

"I'm glad you came out with me."

He was just about to tell her about his day when they were interrupted by the sight of a group of people being led to a nearby table. Kevin's eyes widened as he recognized his parents and the McKinleys.

Missy glanced in their direction. "Aren't those your parents and the McKinleys?"

He stood up abruptly as his mother neared. "I didn't know they were going to be here," he mumbled under his breath.

He obviously didn't speak quietly enough. "We didn't know you were going here, either," his mom said pertly when she caught his accusing tone.

His dad and Mr. and Mrs. McKinley sauntered over to join them. Kevin quickly said a prayer, hoping that they would not join them. After a brief exchange of greetings, the parents gazed at them fondly.

"How is your date going, dear?" Mrs. McKinley asked.

Kevin felt as if he were an eight-year-old again. "Just fine, thank you."

"Did you two go to the movies?"

"Yes, ma'am," he said automatically.

Marianne McKinley wrinkled her nose. "Wasn't it that war movie?"

Missy nodded. "Yes, but it was very exciting."

Baron McKinley looked pleased. "See, Marianne. I told you we should have gone there this evening."

"We lost our bridge game tonight," Daphne explained apologetically. "Baron's not happy."

"We just needed one more point," Baron groused.

Kevin listened to them with only half an ear. Obviously his quiet moment with Missy had passed. Kevin stole a glance at Missy, wondering what she thought of the two couples, bickering like teenagers. She looked content to have the two couples stand by her side all night. He wasn't feeling as generous, however. "Well . . . ," he said, meaningfully.

His father didn't seem to take the hint. "My, you look very nice, Missy. It's nice to see you again."

"Thank you," she answered pleasantly. "It's nice to see you, as well."

Kevin gestured toward their menus. "We were just

about to order," he lied, hoping Missy wouldn't correct him.

"Oh, really?" Daphne asked, as Kevin warily watched his mother eye the vacant pair of seats. "We were just about to sit down," she said, stating the obvious.

Kevin smiled tightly. "Well, then, don't let us keep you."

The two couples shared a grin. "All right, dear. I get the message." Daphne chuckled. "We'll leave you two alone."

Finally the group of parents stepped away. "I'm sorry," he said, sitting down with a small shake of his head. "I promise I didn't know they were going to be here."

Missy looked amused. "I didn't mind seeing them at all, Kevin. They make me laugh the way they carry on."

Chagrined, he said, "That's an apt description. Sometimes they get a little carried away."

She laughed. "They're great."

He had to admit she was right. As much as he liked to complain about them, he wouldn't want to be without his parents for the world.

"I think they're really nice." Her eyes twinkled as she continued. "You looked so funny when they stood here, almost as if you were standing guard."

Embarrassed, he realized that he must have. "I guess I did." He glanced in his parents' direction. They were seated only three tables away. Baron McKinley's gruff voice echoed through the room as he ordered a cocktail. "I never know what they're going to do next. When Baron and my dad decided to host Cameron and Mary Beth's engagement party, they dragged out every baby picture they could find and had them enlarged. All during the party, slides kept appearing on the wall of Mary Beth and Cameron from when they were babies."

"That sounds cute."

"It would have been except most of the pictures were of them naked, in tubs, on rugs . . . all larger than life." Kevin let out a low whistle. "Cam got grief for weeks about those photos."

"I'll try to remember never to mention baby pictures around Mary Beth."

Kevin laughed. "My parents keep busy too. I never know where or when they're going to show up."

"Well, I know that they're planning to go to the Civil War dance, so be prepared."

"They can't wait for that. I'm glad you like them. I guess you're destined to be around the Reece family a lot, in one way or another."

Her eyes sparkled. "You say that like it's a bad thing."

"It's not . . . well, not really," he said truthfully. "I guess I'm suspicious of their presence because they have a bad habit of interfering in their children's lives."

"Really? Whenever your mother speaks about you, it's always in glowing terms. She's really proud of you, Kevin."

He squirmed. "She is, of my job and everything . . . but she hasn't been too happy with my social life lately." He mentally chastised himself as he said the words. He certainly hadn't meant to share that tidbit with Missy.

She cupped her chin with her hands and leaned forward. "Why's that?"

He laughed. "I guess I better rephrase that. My mom hasn't been too happy with my lack of social life. I work more than anything else."

Missy said nothing, only waited quietly for him to continue. Kevin felt honor bound to explain himself. "I've just been so busy, trying to get noticed at work, trying for that next big promotion, and the one after that, and the one after that. Sometimes I feel like the last ten years have gone by without me. I guess you think that's ridiculous, huh?"

"Actually, I'm having pangs of jealousy! I feel like the last ten years have gone by quickly too . . . only I have nothing to show for it." She leaned back. "You should be proud of yourself, Kevin, not ashamed. I don't think anybody can do it all."

He glanced at her for a moment, then turned his attention to his menu. They were a little too close to an exposed nerve for his comfort. "We better go ahead and order. Do you have any idea what you would like?"

Missy shook her head. "No, but I've been advised to have both an appetizer and dessert."

"From Joanne?"

"Of course."

"That sounds like my sister, all right. Well, I hope you do."

They ordered, then chatted about work, the weather, and the movie they had seen.

After a while, their entrees came. Missy thanked the waiter and smiled with pleasure when she gazed at her serving of trout. Kevin picked up his fork, then waited a moment before taking a bite of his steak. "You okay?"

Her head popped up. "Oh, yes, it looks great. I'm just savoring it, I guess."

"What do you mean?"

"Well, this is the nicest dinner I've ever been to. I guess I just don't want it to go by without appreciating it."

His heart went out to her, she had been through so much and still kept a positive attitude. "How about I promise that it won't be the last?"

Her lips curved upward. "All right."

They were quiet then, for a few moments. Kevin was happy just to watch Missy eat.

A burst of laughter exploded into the room. His parents were amused about something. Missy looked in their direction and grinned. "Have your parents known the McKinleys very long?"

"No, only a few years. As you know, the McKinleys are Mary Beth's parents. Mary Beth married my brother Cameron two years ago."

"They're lucky that they all hit it off."

Kevin laughed. "Sometimes I think they are. Other times, well, I wish they didn't get along quite so well. They can be quite an intimidating force when they're all together. My parents have even become more assertive since they've begun their friendship. Now, very few things escape their notice."

Missy chuckled. "Obviously even your nights out, hmm?"

Finally seeing the humor in their situation, Kevin laughed. "I guess so. Even my nights out." He was in no hurry to spend his evening talking about them though. He redirected their conversation to Missy's project.

"It's pretty exciting, really. The building, while not even close to being called condemned, is pretty run-down. It's my job to get it up to par with some of the other historical buildings in the area, in a limited amount of time."

"I can understand that, but why a whole Civil War–themed dance?"

"Joanne and some of the ladies in Payton think it will be a great fund-raiser for the historical society. We're planning to have an annual dance, commemorating Payton's Founder's Day. It will also encourage others to take an interest in other old buildings around town, especially in the downtown civic square."

"Like Joanne's Underground Railroad house."

Missy nodded. "Exactly. I think Joanne's really worried that someone is going to tear down an old house or building without checking into the historical significance of it."

Something in her even tone alerted him that she didn't completely share Joanne's enthusiasm on the subject. "How do you feel about it?"

A bemused smile crossed her features. "Well, it *is* my job. . . ."

"But. . . ."

"But. . . ." She paused for a moment, her eyes glancing toward the ceiling as she obviously tried to put her thoughts into the right words. "But, I guess I just never had the luxury of caring about an old building, Kevin. I was always just trying to get by. I still am, truthfully. I've lived in old, run-down places all my life. I've never been able to romanticize faulty plumbing, or drafty windows, or broken shutters."

"I know what you mean . . . sometimes it's nice just to be able to pick up things and know that they'll work."

Missy laughed. "I'll say. Just once, I'd like to be the first person to use a kitchen appliance, or buy a piece of furniture that's brand-new . . . to use something that's sparkling clean!"

"All antiques don't hold the same appeal, huh?"

She grinned at his statement. "Definitely not. There are times when I definitely pine for something new and shiny!"

He smiled at her wistful tone. "Such as. . . ."

Her eyes widened. "Let's see . . . a toaster, or new salad bowls, or even a new car!"

The list made him laugh. "That's quite an eclectic list!"

"Yes, it is, but don't tell Joanne. As far as she's concerned, I'm with her one hundred percent."

He reached across the table, his gaze catching hers, and said softly, "I wouldn't dream of it."

Chapter Eleven

Missy knew things were too good to be true. Here she was, sitting on the luxurious leather upholstery of Kevin's Lexus, wearing a stylish dress, and going home after dinner at a four-star restaurant. As Kevin took her hand, she tried to imagine that this was just the first of many nights like this. Yeah, right. Girls like her just didn't do things like this. Sooner or later, Kevin was sure to realize that, right?

And when that day came, she would force herself to be grateful to have had even one night like this . . . where she felt special and polished. She could get used to eating her meals alone again. Lord knew that she had recovered from much worse.

"You okay?" Kevin asked, interrupting her thoughts.

"Hmm?" she asked distractedly, then refocused herself to speak like she actually had something to say. "Yes, this is so nice. I was just thinking about what a nice time I've had tonight."

He squeezed her hand. "Me too. We'll have to plan to do this again sometime."

She felt her cheeks warm, like he had read her thoughts. "I'd like that."

All too soon, they were back at her place, and he was walking around the car to open her door. Even though it was an old-fashioned gesture, Missy savored the thrill of it. Somehow it symbolized how the entire evening had been for her. Special. She felt feminine, and giddy, and powerful for that minute . . . like she was worth the trouble . . . like she deserved to have doors opened for her on a regular basis.

And when he opened the door, and reached for her hand, she felt the same tingling rush pass between them. He clasped her hand tightly as she exited the car and stood beside him.

The air had turned cold; she was glad when Kevin folded an arm around her shoulders and brought her close to him. Then it felt only natural to lay her cheek against the soft wool of his coat, his heat warming her heart and spirit.

They slowly walked up her steps, where he took her key from her and unlocked the front door. Finally they stepped into the entryway, illuminated by a dim glow from the lights on the porch.

She turned to him, drawn toward his tender expression and woodsy cologne. Carefully she scanned his features, afraid he was about to disappear from her life like the carriage in *Cinderella*. The outline of his cheekbones cast shadows onto the planes of his face. She was tempted to trace the lines they made with her finger, but he stepped closer and took her hands before she could act on the impulse.

"I had a nice time tonight, Miss," he said, brushing his lips against her cheek.

"Me too," she murmured, savoring his simple gesture. "Thank you again."

He nodded in response, then raised his hands and folded her into his arms. She willingly molded her body to his, reveling in his warmth.

"We'll have to go out again soon, before next Saturday," he said softly between feather-light kisses against her neck. "I don't think I can wait another week."

His words affected her even more than his kisses. Her breath caught. "All right."

Gently, he tilted her head back, his eyes serious as he caught her gaze. "Promise?"

Her pulse raced. What could she say to that? She only nodded. Then slowly, like in a silent movie, she saw his face lower to hers, and feeling brave, she reached up and met him halfway. His lips brushed against hers lightly, then again with more force. His hand brushed across her body, then settled on her face, tracing the outline of her jaw.

Missy held onto him tightly. One hand snaked up to run her fingers through his hair. Kevin deepened the kiss.

Had she ever felt like this before? she wondered through her haze. Had she ever felt this rush of pleasure before, of fierce longing for someone? Had she ever felt so treasured with Scott? Even back when they dated? She honestly couldn't remember.

But then she was drawn back to the man in her arms.

"Goodnight, Miss," he said, raising his head several minutes later. "I better let you go."

She looked into his eyes; they had darkened with passion. She could barely discern the rim of blue around their edges. Instinctively, she knew that he had been just as affected as she by their embrace.

"Sleep well," he said, fingering a long strand of her hair and then watching it fall to her shoulder. "I'll call you tomorrow."

"All right."

He turned from her and walked out the door. As she watched him stride down her steps, she was conscious of how much she already missed his presence. When he got into his car, she closed her eyes, enjoying his scent as it lingered in the air.

She finally closed the door and wandered up the stairs, already wishing that her dream date wasn't over.

* * *

And she was thankful to have the wonderful memory several days later when she was surrounded by Daphne Reece, an army of volunteers, and thirteen yards of gold fabric. With only fourteen days remaining until the dance, the women were in a hurry to get the curtains done and move on to the next items on their lists.

An ironing board, scissors, measuring tapes, and a dish of pins surrounded Missy, along with a bunch of chatter. While she enjoyed the women's enthusiasm, part of her wished she could tell them to lower their voices, like she did to the middle school kids on the museum tours.

But it wasn't meant to be. There was a party atmosphere in the room, and Daphne seemed determined to capture Missy in it.

"What do you think about simple tiebacks, Miss?" Daphne said, holding up the fabric against the window haphazardly.

"I think they will be just fine," she said.

"Maybe a valance? I know we had decided against valances, but they might work if we kept the top of them puffy . . . what do you think?"

She just wanted it done! "Um, a tieback I think."

Daphne grinned. "Me too." She removed the fabric from the window and called to the two women at the sewing machines. "We're staying with Plan A," she called out.

"Gotcha," Mrs. Webster called back, then proceeded to call directions to other women.

Missy shook her head in wonder. Somehow she felt like she was the captain of a mutinous ship. Her crew was moving forward in overdrive and she just hoped that she could keep up. Carefully, she scanned the notepad on her lap and groaned inwardly. Her to-do list took up the whole page, and only the first three items had been crossed off.

"I've already ordered the buffet tables and chairs from the rental company. Have you begun to organize the menu?"

Daphne nodded. "Marianne and I created a phone tree two days ago and assigned dishes. We just need to make sure that someone is here two hours before the party to collect them."

"I'm planning to be here."

"Denise is too."

"And the brochures?" Missy asked.

Daphne had an answer for that also. "Joanne interviewed a family who actually knew some information about the dances that the officers held here. She's going to type up a flyer to pass out to our guests."

Marianne McKinley approached and continued where her best friend had left off. "As you know, I've been in charge of the invitations and reply cards. So far I've received twenty-eight back, each with the forty-dollar donation enclosed."

"That doesn't seem like too many . . . we sent out one hundred and thirty."

Marianne waved a hand. "Don't worry. The RSVP

date isn't for five more days. I'm confident that the reply cards will come pouring in this weekend. People are excited about this party."

"When Jim and I had dinner at the country club, it was all anyone could talk about," Daphne interjected.

Missy couldn't help but shake her head in wonder. "I am just amazed at how much we've gotten done. Thank goodness I called you!"

Marianne sat down on the floor next to Missy, pulling her wool slacks into a neat fold as she crossed her legs. "I'm so glad you did." She shared a look with Daphne. "We're thinking that you and Joanne need to host a dance every year. It's been a lot of fun."

Missy groaned in mock horror. "I think we're planning on it, but to be honest with you, I don't know if I can do this again."

Daphne chuckled at Missy's expression. "Sure you can, you're a natural!"

For the next two hours, the women worked steadily. Missy helped wherever she could, and felt very professional when she took calls on her new cell phone. Joanne had persuaded her to borrow it during the project; Missy was glad that she had taken her up on the offer. In the past two hours, she had taken calls from a variety of people, from carpenters to rental companies, along with several phone calls from Joanne, who was holding down things at the museum.

Finally, at five-thirty, it was time to stop for the day. As the women collected their purses and gear, Missy made a concerted effort to thank each one for their time. Most just clasped her hands and told her that it had been fun.

Daphne looked at Missy fondly when she pulled on her jacket. "So, do you have plans for this evening?"

Missy shook her head with a smile. "No, thank goodness. I'm just going to catch a bite at The Grill and then collapse at home."

Daphne nodded in understanding. "Fund-raising is an underappreciated art, I believe."

Missy had to agree with her assessment. "Thanks again. I'm really looking forward to seeing our finished product. And the city council has even made plans to host a dinner in this room next month."

"Things are coming together. I hope it gets a lot of publicity. I need to call the papers again, to make sure they plan to cover it."

"I'm relieved you're taking care of that." Missy laughed. "I don't think I'm quite ready to deal with reporters."

Daphne stepped toward the door, then stopped. "Kevin made me promise to keep my mouth shut . . . but, ah . . . did you have a good time the other night at The Cork?"

"Very nice. It's a beautiful restaurant."

Daphne nodded. "It was good to see you there . . . with Kevin," she finished choppily. "He's been really happy lately."

Missy swallowed. "I'm glad."

"I'm just so pleased that you're dating him," Daphne said, then guiltily covered her mouth with her palm. "Oh, don't tell him I said a word! He'd be so mad."

Eyes shining, Missy said, "I won't tell a soul, I promise."

"Thanks. Um, has Kevin or Joanne mentioned the baby shower that we're giving for Cameron and Mary Beth?"

"Joanne has once or twice." Or thirty times, Missy thought privately.

"I hope you're planning to come?"

She was actually looking forward to it. "I am, it should be a lot of fun."

"Oh, it will be," Daphne said cryptically before glancing at her watch in alarm. "Oh, gosh, I better go. Jim wants to go to the club tonight. Bye, dear."

"Bye, Mrs. Reece, and thanks again."

Then, with a wave of her hand, Daphne Reece was off, her heels clicking down the stairs.

Now that the room was empty, Missy turned to inspect the progress. Already it looked completely different than it had two short weeks ago. The wood floor gleamed; the walls were a deep Victorian red. The plumbers had already inspected the bathrooms and the mini-kitchen in the back and found everything in surprising working order. Tomorrow, carpenters were due to arrive to replace the worn Formica.

She wandered around the room, previous conversations echoing through her head. Wreaths were being made to adorn the walls. Memorabilia was being framed in Plexiglas shadowboxes for the big night. Art students were painting banners for the street and the outside of the building. A few men who had experience with sound systems were going to string wire on Saturday.

The curtains were being sewn. She planned to paint baseboards early next week. And, as soon as the light fixtures worked again, everything would be practically ready.

Not for the first time, she wondered what the large room had looked like so long ago, in 1866, with scared soldiers and women inhabiting the building. Had they even bothered with decorations back then?

Did they bother with invitations and reply cards, with glossy woodwork and sparkling windows?

Had it even mattered if there was enough food or wine?

She didn't think so.

Absently, she raised her hands and twirled in the center of the floor, pretending to waltz with a handsome soldier. She hummed a lazy tune, her feet moving in rhythm.

Again her mind drifted. What had the atmosphere been like during those dances? Noisy? Rowdy? Bittersweet?

What had people talked about? The war? Their beliefs? Anything but? How would she have acted, knowing that her partner was about to leave to an uncertain future?

She could imagine strong arms circling her waist, the uniform's scratchy wool under her elbow-length gloves. The catch in her breath as she realized that everything she cherished could be taken away.

Her steps slowed.

What if her soldier had been Kevin? What would she have done? Would she have clung to him, begged him to be careful? Put on a brave face and told him that she would be just fine?

Memories of his embrace came flooding back. She closed her eyes as she recalled their last kiss. His expression had been so tender, his lips so responsive. She had felt feminine and desirable in his arms. How could she have let him go off to war?

Suddenly a horn beeped outside and she was startled out of her reverie. Her eyes opened in shock.

The room was empty. Boxes, paint cans, and yards of fabric littered the floor. It smelled of turpentine, fresh paint, and furniture polish. In fourteen days, she'd be having a party in this room, ready or not.

Her notepad lay open by the door, waiting for her attention.

Suddenly, it was too much to ponder. She needed to get out of there. Quickly, Missy grabbed her belongings and set off for some dinner, more than ready for some well-deserved peace and quiet.

Chapter Twelve

When Missy arrived at The Grill, she observed the crowd, but was disappointed to find that it didn't lift her spirits as it normally did. Usually it was bursting with people: teenagers grabbing a snack before dinner, moms getting something cool to drink after taking the kids to the nearby park . . . others, like her, who ate when they were hungry, and not at designated mealtimes.

Missy liked to go to The Grill after work, when she had nothing else planned to do. It was nice to remember the times she spent working there and catch up on news with the manager. Some nights, it was just nice to go there and be with others, instead of her empty duplex.

But lately, her life had been the opposite of boring.

Exciting and breathless were more apt words to describe it. And, even though she enjoyed the minor chaos, she felt the need to do something familiar, something over which she was in complete control. Between her job and Kevin, and the whole Reece family . . . lately there had been no time to just luxuriate in her privacy. She smiled at the term. When had that happened? When had she started to crave time alone?

She sipped her diet soda again, enjoyed the feeling of being alone with her thoughts, and scanned the crowd from her table in the middle of the room. It was a rare day when she didn't recognize anyone—but that was the case today.

A young mom with her toddler sat to her left, the little boy seemed more interested in throwing his French fries on the floor than into his mouth.

An elderly couple sat a few tables away, both eating grilled cheese sandwiches in comfortable silence, and a rather pudgy, distinguished-looking man was seated at the table in front of her, talking a mile a minute on a cell phone and munching on a hot dog every time he paused for a breath. Missy couldn't help but watch him out of the corner of her eyes. He spoke loudly . . . there seemed to be a problem with the heater in his office . . . and she could only imagine what his life was like if he couldn't even relax for ten minutes to eat his dinner.

Then he stopped talking. A strange, gurgling sound came from his throat. Surprised, Missy directed her whole gaze toward him. He was holding his throat and looked alarmed. Quickly, she looked around for help, but nobody else seemed aware of his predicament. He stood up, gasping for air. Then, before she realized what she was doing, Missy ran over to him.

He looked a little purplish. "Sir? Sir, are you all right?"

His only response was a weak gasp and a bewildered expression. Automatically, she pulled him towards her, arranged her arms under his ribcage like she had seen on the Discovery Channel, made a fist with her two hands, and squeezed upwards on what she hoped was his diaphragm two times.

Just like in a cartoon, a piece of hot dog popped out of his open mouth, followed by a huge gasp for air.

She and the man looked at each other in shock. The Heimlich maneuver really worked! It was hard to believe that she, Missy Schuler, had just saved this man's life! "You all right, sir?" she asked again. He just looked at her, stunned and silent.

Suddenly realizing that the other occupants in the restaurant had circled around them, Missy turned to the young mom she had noticed before. "Do you think we should call 911?"

The woman gestured to the cell phone sitting on the top of her stroller. "I just did, although I think you saved him already." She looked at Missy with admiration. "That was pretty amazing to watch. You were so calm, cool, and collected. Thank goodness you were here!"

The praise, spoken out loud, seemed excessive. "I just did what anyone. . . ."

"Thank you," the man rasped.

Startled, Missy turned to him. He looked weak and shaken, but his color was slowly coming back. "You're very welcome," she replied with a smile.

Just then a blare of sirens broke the silence, followed by the appearance of two EMT's. Everyone began talking at once. Missy stood quietly, content to let the others explain the situation and the man describe how he was feeling.

Shaken, she curved her arms around her middle and tried not to think about what could have happened if the Heimlich hadn't worked.

She was startled out of her reverie by the policeman who had been writing notes. "Well, Missy Schuler," he said with a grin. "How does it feel to have saved a United States congressman's life?"

Her eyes widened. "I'm sorry?"

"This man is Congressman Zeiler."

Missy turned to the congressman in astonishment. Color had finally returned to his face, and he looked almost distinguished again. "How's that for doing your civic duty, young lady?" He chortled.

"I'm just glad I was there to help," she said.

"Me too, me too."

After a few moments, the policemen and George,

the local newspaper reporter, surrounded the two. Missy scanned the small crowd around her in surprise. News sure did travel fast in a small town. Missy had known George since grade school, and within minutes she was answering questions about her quick thinking. That flowed into a description of her job, and finally a plug for the Civil War dance.

Congressman Zeiler seemed content to let her do most of the speaking. She realized that he was letting her have the spotlight.

Finally, an hour later, they were alone again. Missy stood up, uncomfortable now with the man's steady gaze on her. Just as she was about to tell him good-bye, creases appeared around his mouth and eyes as he broke into a wide grin. "Thanks again."

She fidgeted. He had already thanked her several times. "You're welcome."

He motioned toward George, who they could see pulling out of the parking lot. "That dance of yours sounds like quite an undertaking."

She couldn't help but grin at the description. He didn't know the half of it. "I'll say. It's exciting, though. I'm proud to have the responsibility."

He nodded, his eyes darting to the parking lot. Missy had a feeling that he had just spied her old Taurus. "Is there anything I can do to repay you, Miss Schuler?"

She blushed. She was strapped for money, but things weren't so bad that she was reduced to making money off of other people's misfortunes! "Definitely not. I promise, I was just glad to help."

"Now, hold on, it's not everybody who puts themselves out like that. I'd appreciate it if there was some way that I could show my appreciation."

Missy had to smile. From some people, she imagined his offer of appreciation might sound like a proposition. But Congressman Zeiler made it sound like the kind of offer one made when you weren't used to getting anything without a lot of finagling. She thought over her reply, then came up with the perfect compensation. "Well, if you would like to repay me, you could come to our Civil War dance."

His eyes twinkled. "That's it?"

"I know you're a busy man. But, your appearance would mean a lot and would also add support to what we've been preaching: that the history of Payton is worth saving and appreciating."

His kind gaze held hers for a moment longer, then he reached into his pocket and pulled out two business cards. "Call me, or write me and let me know the particulars. If I'm in town, I'll definitely come. But no matter what, my wife Patsy and I will lend our support."

Missy took the proffered cards and then shook his hand. "Thanks, Congressman Zeiler."

The next morning, Joanne met her with a bouquet of flowers and a Cheshire-cat grin. "I hear I have a bona fide hero working for me now."

Already she could feel her cheeks heating as she took the bouquet. "Hardly. Uh, who are the flowers from?"

"Congressman Zeiler." At Missy's look of surprise, Joanne grinned impishly. "The florist told me when she delivered them."

Missy smelled the blooms. "They're lovely."

Joanne nodded. "They are—and perfect for my illustrious assistant."

"Ha, ha."

"Well, at least a local celebrity! You looked good on the front page of the paper this morning."

The memory of the flashing lights and microphone made Missy shudder anew. "I can't believe how this whole thing has been blown out of proportion. I didn't do anything that anybody else wouldn't have done."

Joanne's grin widened. "But nobody else did," she pointed out.

Missy only shrugged.

Joanne toyed with the end of her pencil. "By the way, Stratton said that you did everything right. How did you learn to do that?"

"On the Discovery Channel."

"Just from watching TV?"

"It looked interesting, but I never thought I'd actually have to do it."

"Congressman Zeiler seems appreciative."

This time it was Missy's turn to smile serenely. "He was."

Joanne tilted her head. "What does that mean?"

"It means that he's so appreciative that he's going to try to come to our Memorial Building dance," she said triumphantly.

Joanne's jaw dropped. "Really?"

"Really." Missy beamed. "And if he can't, he promised to support our efforts to promote interest in our town's history. He gave me two of his cards, and told me to write him about the details of this dance. He was very gracious."

Joanne's eyes glowed happily. "Wow. Can you imagine a United States congressman coming to our dance?" She jumped up and impulsively hugged Missy. "I can't thank you enough."

Missy shrugged. Then, more than ready to concentrate on something besides her newfound heroics, she pointed to a bag of party decorations next to Joanne's desk. "How are things going for Cameron and Mary Beth's baby shower?"

"Really well. I'm so glad that it's going to be a couple shower instead of just women," she commented. "I think Stratton's even getting excited about it. Is Kevin?"

"He hasn't said too much about it, but I'm sure we'll have a good time." They glanced at the clock, and then at the pile of papers on Joanne's desk. "You ready to go through next week's schedule? I've already heard from several volunteers. I think we can begin filling slots."

Joanne picked up her pen, all business. "Let's do it."

They worked hard for the next two hours, first reviewing the volunteer and staff schedules, then moving onto finances. Joanne wrote checks while Missy recorded the expenditures. They had just begun a lengthy inventory of a donation from someone's attic when a deliveryman bearing an armload of flowers interrupted them.

Joanne raised her eyebrows after discovering that the bouquet was for Missy. "You receive more flowers than anyone I know."

"It's a new occurrence, believe me."

She set the bouquet on the corner of Joanne's desk. It was fragrant and beautiful, like one of those bouquet ads on TV. A white envelope was nestled in between a clump of pink roses. She pulled out the enclosed card and then stared at the message.

It looks like it has come around. . . . I'm proud of you.

Love, Kevin

Joanne read the card over Missy's shoulder. "It has come around . . . what does that mean?"

Missy laughed. "When your brother rescued me on the side of the road, I told him that I wouldn't ever know how to repay him. He just said that good deeds go around—that one day I'd find the opportunity to do something nice for someone else, and that that would be repayment enough." She paused, remembering her feelings of inadequacy during the conversation. "Honestly, I didn't believe him. I thought that there was no possible way I could ever do something meaningful for someone else."

Joanne reached out and gently brushed her finger against a pink-hued rose petal. "I'd say you're officially on your own two feet, now, Missy."

She laughed. "Hardly."

Joanne held up a hand and counted off her fingers as she spoke. "Let's see—you've taken over this project with the Memorial Building."

"Only started . . . you may regret it too!"

"And saved a congressman's life."

"Joanne. . . ."

Joanne ignored her. "You're moving on with your life, and finally, you're falling in love again. I'd say things are looking up for you."

Missy opened her mouth to reply, but simply closed it instead. Things certainly were looking up for her. She took a deep breath, and became aware of the surge of pride that she sensed in herself. It felt strange and unfamiliar. But good. "I think I'll go call Kevin," she said simply, instead of trying to convey the jumble of feelings that were bubbling inside her.

Joanne's gray eyes softened. "I think that's a fine idea."

Chapter Thirteen

"I hope you don't mind that that we're going to this baby shower," Kevin said to Missy as he maneuvered the car into the parallel parking spot in front of his sister's home. "There was no way that I could get out of it."

"I don't mind at all. In fact, it sounds like fun. Both your mom and Joanne have already mentioned it several times to me . . . I wouldn't dare miss it. Plus, I promised to bring a dessert."

He looked at the black forest cake she held. It looked delicious, but more importantly, it looked like she was fitting in just fine. He knew his sisters didn't ask casual acquaintances from work to help with meals. Once again he was struck about how his feelings for her had changed from protective to more romantic. He enjoyed being with her, and he wanted her to feel the same way with him, even around his family.

He knew for certain that the group tonight was sure to be good-natured and easygoing. It would be a perfect climate for Missy to feel comfortable. "I promised Cameron and Stratton I'd stop by," Kevin continued. "They both were slightly horrified that this is a 'couple' baby shower."

"And you're not?"

He shifted in his seat. "I am too."

Missy smiled in response. "Well, there will be *two* parents," she said matter-of-factly.

"Oh, I don't think we're squeamish about the parenting thing, it's the other stuff that worries us."

"Such as?"

"Awful baby shower games . . . a girl at work told me all about diapering races and blindfolded baby-food taste tests."

"Gosh, I don't recall Joanne mentioning those," she said, struggling to keep a straight face. "I think this party will center more around gifts."

Kevin grimaced. "Everyone's going to be oohing and ahhing over little baby things. And Cam doesn't relish the thought of every mother there recounting her labor and delivery war stories."

"Your brother-in-law Stratton doesn't mind?"

"As you know, Stratton's a doctor. He could probably tell his own set of war stories if he put his mind to it," Kevin said as they unbuckled their seat belts.

"Of course, it's different when you're talking about a relative."

"I guess so." She laughed. "Well, I'll do my best to redirect any labor conversations."

Kevin grinned. "If you can do that, every guy in there will be indebted to you for life."

"Now that's something to look forward to."

When they reached the brightly lit house, Kevin knocked on the door and then opened it before anyone had a chance to receive them. Immediately they were engulfed in the warmth of his family. He glanced over worriedly as his brothers and parents reacquainted themselves with Missy. She was bombarded with questions about her heroic behavior. Kevin scowled. As usual, his family was aggressive and loud. He had hoped they would be on their best behavior, but he was slowly realizing that they didn't have that. They were strictly a what-you-see-is-what-you-get type of clan.

There was something so fragile about Missy sometimes, almost as though she were holding herself stiffly so she wouldn't break. And, he had also noticed during dinner that she hadn't eaten much of anything. Was she worried about the party?

Or perhaps she was having trouble with work or her finances. For once, he wished that she wasn't working for his sister. Then, he could just drop by and check on her now and then. As it was, he knew if he stopped by unannounced he would get a knowing smirk from Joanne.

He was brought out of his thoughts by a hug from his sister-in-law. Mary Beth looked as cute as ever in leggings and one of Cameron's old college sweat-shirts. Even at seven months pregnant, she looked fresh and young, like a college coed. "I'm glad you both could stop by," she said.

He leaned down to kiss her cheek and give her stomach a pat. "We wouldn't miss it."

"Missy, your cake looks beautiful. Do you want to come back to the kitchen with me to cut it?"

"Sure," Missy replied.

"Thanks." Mary Beth smiled, then rubbed her back wearily. "Would you mind helping me make some coffee too? Joanne was going to make some decaf, but an unexpected guest sidetracked her for a minute."

"I'd love to help," she said, then followed Mary Beth through the living room toward the back of the house.

Kevin watched them walk away and then met the gaze of his brothers Jeremy and Cameron.

"She's cute, Kevin," Cam said.

Kevin thought of how pretty she looked in her crisp white blouse and navy slacks. "I think so too. She's shy though, and kind of quiet."

"She's great," Joanne corrected as she joined them from a room hidden behind the stairs. "Don't worry,

Missy has many talents. She already fits right in with our family. She'll be fine."

"She's just a friend," he felt compelled to add, but too late, because his siblings had already gone ahead into the living room.

Kevin noticed that the room was already decorated and festive-looking. Streamers and balloons were strewn haphazardly. Presents wrapped in pastel colors littered the coffee table and floor in front of a Victorian-style floral couch.

Once again he was struck by the differences in the home from the time Joanne had first championed it. The woodwork gleamed and the atmosphere was cozy, despite the fact that two of the rooms in the back served as a makeshift museum on the history of the home.

It was one of four houses in the county that was a recognized Underground Railroad station during the Civil War. Twice a month Joanne let visitors tour the cellar where slaves had hidden and spoke about the original owners of the home.

For now, the glass French doors that divided the home from the museum were closed and it simply seemed like a cozy home.

Kevin smiled in satisfaction as he watched his brother-in-law Stratton recline lazily against the overstuffed pillows on the couch.

"I thought y'all were going out tonight," Stratton drawled to Kevin as he joined him on the couch.

"We did, for appetizers right after work. I took Missy to The Sleepy Hollow Inn."

Joanne settled herself on the floor in front of her husband and raised her eyebrows at the mention of the famed restaurant. "I love that place. It's so romantic with that big fireplace and those crisp white tablecloths."

Kevin shifted uncomfortably under his sister's knowing gaze. "I don't know about romantic, but the food was good."

"You guys have been seeing each other a lot lately." Cameron eyed his brother. "Didn't you see her for dinner last week too?"

"Yeah, and the week before that she cooked dinner for me."

Joanne smiled in satisfaction. "Oh," she said. After years of being subjected to that one word, Kevin knew exactly what it meant.

"Honestly, Joanne," he began, but was stopped by the entrance of Mary Beth, Missy, and his mother. Missy was holding a tray and listening to his mother chatter on about something. He stood up automatically to help her set the tray on the table.

As their fingers touched, he felt a tremor race up to his wrist. "Thanks," she said simply, and then sat down next to him.

The next hour flew by as more family members and friends of theirs came in and gifts were opened. Baby clothes, bottles, toys, and blankets littered the floor.

Cookies were passed around, along with pieces of the cake that Missy had made. Knowing what was in his refrigerator at home, Kevin helped himself to a little of everything. He noticed that Missy did the same, and even began to shyly participate in the conversations.

The only time he saw her tense up was when Mary Beth opened her last present, the one from her husband Cameron. In a beautifully wrapped box was a long white cotton nightgown, with a large amount of lace and embroidery around the neck and sleeves. Mary Beth had held it up in front of her in awe.

"It's for the hospital, Mary," Cam said, his gaze tender towards his wife.

"Oh, Cam, the baby will probably ruin it," Mary Beth replied.

"It won't matter; you'll still look beautiful, hon," he said.

Kevin, Stratton, and Joanne had felt honor bound to say, "Aahh," together and tease Cam, but Kevin noticed Missy look at the couple with longing in her eyes. He realized that his brother's marriage was obviously vastly different from the way hers had been. He was reminded again of how much she had been through.

For Missy, the evening was a night full of revelations. Although she had been with the Reece family before, now she felt as if she were looking at them through new eyes, with more awareness. What would it be like to be a part of a family like this?

She had never seen her mother look at her with love the way Mrs. Reece did with her husband and kids. And the friendly banter filled her with warmth and joy. It was so nice to be a part of their group, to imagine what it would be like if the Reece family was her own.

They had just been about to leave when she accidentally knocked into Joanne, and Joanne's coffee had spilled across the front of her blouse. Although the liquid wasn't scorching, she gasped from its connection with her skin.

"Oh, I'm so sorry," Joanne blurted.

"It's all right; it wasn't that hot, and I think I bumped into you," Missy replied, although she saw Kevin glancing at her with concern. She glanced down to survey the damage and saw that her white blouse was soaked and that the outline of her bra was clearly visible. Missy scanned the room for the coat that she had been wearing.

"Joanne, go get Missy one of your T-shirts," Mrs. Reece said.

Alarm coursed through her when she imagined what everyone would say if they saw the scars on her bare arm. "No, that's all right," she said earnestly. "I'll be okay until I get home."

But it was as if she had never spoken. "It'll just be a minute, Missy," Joanne urged, smiling. "Come on up with me."

Missy glanced at Kevin. He grinned. "You know, they're going to bug you until you say yes. And it is pretty chilly out there."

He was right. "Okay," she said and followed his sister upstairs.

Ten minutes later she returned, holding her soiled blouse and feeling conspicuous. The sleeves of the shirt stopped at least six inches above her elbow, and she knew her scars would look vivid under the bright lights. Missy felt as if everyone's eyes were automatically drawn to her arms. She pulled her arm closer to her in embarrassment.

She scanned the room for Kevin. He strode towards her, and she saw his features tightening as he approached. She knew the reason for his expression.

Portions of her skin from her elbow to her wrist were pink and puckered, as if someone had twisted it painfully. She wasn't sure how much Kevin had told his family about her marriage and accident, but she assumed that most had at least heard about it. After all, Payton was a small town.

"Hey, Missy, what happened to your arm?" Jeremy said as she approached.

"For goodness sake, Jeremy," Kevin hissed.

"It's all right," she said. It almost felt good for someone to be direct about her scars—to not just look at her in pity.

"It's, ah, a burn. I had an accident a few years ago

and I'm afraid I should have gone to a plastic surgeon or something to get it taken care of properly."

"You know, I've never asked you if it still hurts. Did the burn hurt you?" Joanne asked.

Kevin looked as if he was going to go ballistic. It was a nice change for someone to want to protect her feelings. Missy hid a smile.

"Joanne," he said quietly through clenched teeth, "maybe she doesn't want to talk about this. I'll get your coat, Miss, and we can take off."

But she stopped him with a hand on his arm. "No, it's okay. It doesn't hurt; it's just a little tender. The doctor said that the soreness and scars would fade in time . . . and it really does look much better than it did years ago when it happened."

"Did he give you some Vitamin E oil?" Stratton asked. "Sometimes that can really help with scarring."

Missy shared a smile with the doctor. "I think we all know that nothing is going to make this look much better. And truly, it doesn't bother me. I just try to hide it as best I can."

Kevin held her coat for her. "I think you look fine, Miss," he said gruffly. "Don't worry about it."

But the rest of the family didn't seem daunted by his demeanor.

"Hey, Missy, next time I see you I'll show you my scar," Jeremy teased, playfully lifting up his shirt.

"I have some good ones from bee stings," Cam added.

"Oh, Cam. That's nothing compared to the cut I got when I fell out of a tree when I was five," Mary Beth retorted.

Missy couldn't help herself, she started to laugh. Kevin's family was treating the scars she always tried to hide with shame like battle wounds to be displayed with pride.

And perhaps that's what they were: marks from the hardest battle she had ever fought. She glanced at Kevin and caught the death glare he was sending to his siblings.

Before she could stop herself, she quipped, "Oh, just wait until I show you the matching scars on my thigh . . . then you'll realize your bee stings have nothing on me."

That brought laughter to the group, except from Kevin, who gazed at her in concern.

"It's okay, Kevin," she murmured. "I promise."

Minutes later they left the party and walked out to the car. But before she got in, Kevin drew her lightly into an embrace, and kissed her on the forehead. "I'm sorry," he whispered to her.

"For what?"

"For the scars, for your marriage, for the questions, for everything."

"It's okay, Kevin," she said again, and this time she really meant it. Right now, at this time, things were okay. Right now it didn't matter that she was permanently scarred on various parts of her body. It had felt good to laugh at herself for once, and eat cake, and help fix coffee, and sit across from the most handsome man she had ever met.

It had been a good night. A night worth savoring. And she had learned from past experience to treasure these moments. After all, she hadn't had too many of them.

Chapter Fourteen

"You going home, Missy?" Kathleen, one of the volunteers, asked as she and Missy were putting on their coats in the staff room at the museum.

Missy smiled tiredly at the elderly lady who had volunteered in the museum gift shop for as long as she could remember. "Not yet. I need to head on over to the third floor for a while."

"Lots to do?"

"Too much," Missy agreed. "But in a little over a week it will all be over and I'll miss the excitement, I'm sure."

"I know the feeling. I used to feel the same way after performing plays in high school," Kathleen said wistfully. "There's just something about accomplishing a big goal that gets your adrenaline flowing."

"I wish someone would tell that to the circles under my eyes." Missy chuckled.

Kathleen smiled at the remark, her weathered face crinkling in amusement. "For what it's worth, I think you're doing a good job. In fact, I heard Joanne say she was impressed by your professionalism."

Hearing about the praise from Joanne gave Missy a welcome feeling of satisfaction. "Thanks for telling me. Sometimes I feel that I'm trying to do too much and end up not doing any of it well. During today's tour, I was sure the Native American display was never going to be the same after those little five-year-olds took an interest in the pottery."

"Once I had a first-grader who decided he needed to take a break. He fell asleep on the antique Shaker bed upstairs. No one could find him for thirty minutes!" Kathleen laughed. "Crazy things have happened to all of us here. It builds character." She opened the door. "I'll see you tomorrow."

"Bye," Missy replied, then locked the doors behind her and walked out to her car.

There were some days when she felt she had earned every penny of her salary, and today had been one of them. There was a running joke among the volunteers that it was a toss-up between which was worse, kindergarteners or sixth-graders. Since she had had the dubious pleasure of escorting both groups that day, she felt she could say with confidence that the smart-mouthed older ones could give those touchy-feely five-year-olds a run for their money.

Now, added to her workload were the multitude of preparations for the dance. Mrs. Reece and a few of her friends had helped address fifty flyers for shops around town, and the next day was going to be spent in old clothes, painting the baseboards and trim a creamy white. In addition, she needed to organize the delivery schedules for the bar, glassware, tables and chairs, and stage for the band.

Missy also knew that Joanne had been giving several speeches to clubs around town in order to further advertise for the program. And even Congressman Zeiler, bless his heart, had gotten into the act by granting an interview with the Cincinnati newspaper about the importance of showcasing their town's unusual history.

With all that in mind, Missy was doubly glad that 6:00 had arrived. A cool breeze met her as she walked toward her car. She stood motionless for a moment, savoring the refreshing burst of air before climbing into her car. Honestly, it felt as if it was never going to warm up this year. The damp March wind seeped into her bones every time she walked outdoors. Thank goodness April was just around the corner.

She continued thinking about the weather and her list of things to do as she made the short trek to the Memorial Building. Within minutes, she had climbed the three flights of stairs and was fiddling with the old locks yet again.

As soon as she entered she turned on the lights and got to work. The trim around the doors needed another coat of paint. And, if she had time, she wanted to continue organizing the cabinets in the back of the room. The volunteers had brought cleaning supplies, toiletries, and basic kitchenware for the kitchen and storage area. It would be good to finally have a place to put it all.

Missy turned on an oldies station on a boom box that Joanne had brought in, pulled her hair back in a messy knot, and sang along. After a while, the heat in the building kicked in full blast and she pulled off her sweater, cooling off in just the T-shirt she had worn underneath. Two hours had passed when she heard footsteps on the stairs.

Startled, she stared at the door, then sighed in relief when Kevin appeared. "Hey," she said. "How did you know I was here?"

He walked forward, carrying a sack from a local fast-food restaurant. "I saw your car in the parking lot on my way home from my parents."

"I'm glad you stopped by," she said, taking in his dark suit and overcoat.

He gave a smile that didn't quite reach his eyes, then situated himself next to her on the floor. "What are you doing here?"

She waved a hand at the open paint can and shiny

woodwork. "What do you think I'm doing?" she said with a smile. But he wasn't smiling back. He looked irritated and worried.

"I mean," he said slowly, "what are you doing here at eight at night by yourself?"

"Painting."

"Don't you think it's time to call it a day?"

She shook her head. "Not a chance. I promised Joanne that I'd have quite a bit done for her by tomorrow. I've still got at least another hour and a half to go."

Concern clouded his face. "Why don't you just finish up tomorrow morning?"

What was going on with him? "Because I have other things that need to be done tomorrow, Kevin. I told Joanne that I'd sit in on a grant meeting for her."

His eyes darkened. "Where is she, anyway?"

Missy shrugged. "I think she's home. She left work early today."

His lips tightened as he handed her the sack. "I brought you a burger. Have you eaten?"

"No, I forgot." She unwrapped the sandwich and bit into it gratefully. "I was going to grab something on my way over, but I started to talk to one of our volunteers and forgot all about it."

If anything, that made Kevin look even more annoyed. "What's wrong?" she asked. Maybe his new position at work was not going well.

"I just think you need to take better care of yourself,

Miss. I know this is the second time this week that you've gone to the museum all day and then here afterward. I hate to see you doing so much. You're going to wear yourself out."

"But this is my job," she reminded him. "I'm sure you've worked plenty of late nights without anyone complaining."

"That's different."

"How so?" she snapped.

He waved a hand. "I needed to get the accounts in order to get this promotion."

She put her sandwich down. "Well, Kevin Reece, I need the *money* from all of this overtime that I've been working to pay my bills. And, I need to show Joanne that I can do the things that she's asking of me."

"Well, I think she's being unreasonable and demanding." He sighed, then reached out to brush a strand of hair behind her ear. "Look, why don't you let me call her? I'll tell Joanne that you've put in enough hours today," he murmured. "Then, I'll take you home." His expression softened. "We can watch a movie on TV."

Even though she knew that Kevin had the best of intentions, his words rubbed her the wrong way. Never again was she going to let someone tell her what was best for her. "Don't you dare call *my* boss and tell her that."

"Missy, you're being dramatic. We're talking about Joanne here."

She tried to breathe evenly, but it was hard. "You don't seem to understand that I have things to do that are important to me, that need to be done."

"I understand that you're exhausted and that you're up here by yourself, at night."

Oh, why could he not understand what she was saying? The last thing she needed was him hovering. "I appreciate your concern," she said as she stood up. "But you better leave."

"What?"

"I don't have the energy or time to fight with you right now."

Kevin scowled at her. "Honestly, Missy. . . ."

"I've got a thousand things to do, none of which can get done while I'm sitting here with you," she said seriously. "And furthermore, the last thing I need today is your patronizing attitude."

"Patronizing?" he retorted. "I'm just trying to take care of you."

It seemed like this was her week to stand up for herself. "Kevin, I want to *date* you, not hire you as my mother. It's bad enough that I work for your sister, and that I'm far, far below you on the social scale. But you're not going to be able to enter my life and single-handedly patch it up like this building. Just be supportive of me—at least let me have some dignity."

"I am not seeing you just to fix your problems."

She met his gaze head-on. "Then why are you?"

He waited too long to reply.

"It's that tough, huh?" Wearily she brushed a stray strand of hair away from her eyes. "Well, that's just great. Good night, Kevin." She walked over to the door and held it open for him. Reluctantly he walked to the threshold.

But before he descended the staircase, he turned around. "Missy. . . ."

She forced herself to be strong. "Good night, Kevin."

He sighed. "May I call you?"

She waited three beats before replying. "You may."

Finally he left.

She stood motionless as she heard his footsteps fade away down the stairs. What had happened to her lately? Where was the shy girl no one ever paid attention to? She felt strange and unfamiliar as she pondered her new life.

She was shouldering a lot of responsibility and had the complete faith of her director that she would be successful; she was saving the lives of important men and bossing around society ladies; she was making new friends and giggling over dates and outfits, just like she had wished she could do in high school.

And, she had told off the first man who genuinely cared about her . . . the man who only wanted to shelter her and put her on a pedestal. She had forced the man she was falling in love with to leave her alone. What had she done?

Of course, she had done the right thing. Kevin

needed to begin to treat her as an equal if they were ever to have a satisfying, real relationship. Pity and support were two entirely different things. He needed to realize that.

Had she told him that? Her lips twisted as she tried to recall their conversation. What *had* she said? She couldn't remember exactly . . . just that it was a particularly feisty conversation.

Now completely disgruntled, she turned to the one thing that seemed to be going well: her painting. Sighing, Missy picked back up her paintbrush and went back to work.

She *would* get this job done and Joanne *would* be proud of her. And more importantly, she would be proud of herself.

Chapter Fifteen

Kevin slammed his hand on the steering wheel as he drove away from the Memorial Building. Where did she get off, sending him away? After all, he was the good guy in the situation; he was the one trying to help her out. And all he got in return was a lecture about interfering with her efforts to improve herself. Didn't she realize that the time to build confidence was not late at night, working herself to the bone?

And that led him to think about his sister Joanne. Since when had she become such a slave driver, anyway? How could she just assign Missy those jobs and not even offer to help her out? Nothing made sense.

Although he knew he was probably making things worse, he turned left at the stop sign instead of right, and made his way to Joanne's home. Hopefully

Joanne's husband Stratton would be there also, and would serve to mediate their conversation, because Kevin knew it wouldn't be pretty.

He was thinking about the few choice words he would say to her when Stratton opened the door and let him in. "Hey, Kevin," he said. "I didn't know you were stopping by. I was just cleaning up the kitchen."

"I need to speak with Joanne."

Stratton's blue eyes narrowed as he stepped back and allowed him entrance. "Come on in, then."

"Who's here?" Joanne called, then stopped by the foot of the stairs when she saw who had arrived. "Oh, it's you."

Kevin seethed, and was almost thankful for Joanne's rude words. It made his reply that much easier to say. "Joanne, you've got a lot of nerve."

A hand went to her hip. "Is that right?"

"I just came from your dance hall building. Missy's there, working late again, to get all of your work done."

Joanne looked pleased. "That's great. I promised some of the board members that they could visit tomorrow."

He saw red. "Is that all you have to say? I can't believe that you're making her do everything while you're here, sitting around the house."

Joanne stepped forward. "Exactly what, Kevin, am I supposed to be saying right now?"

Stratton closed the front door. "Listen, Kevin," he

said quietly. "You need to settle down. There's no call for you to come barging into this house and flinging accusations."

"They aren't accusations; they're facts," he corrected, then turned to his sister again. "You, of all people, should know how fragile Missy is, Joanne. I can't believe you're treating her this way."

Joanne arched an auburn eyebrow. "Fragile? She's a grown woman."

"Oh, for pete's sake, Joanne, you know what I mean."

Stratton stepped forward. "Enough, Kevin. I'll not have you upsetting Joanne right now. Go into the kitchen."

"Oh, really?" Kevin said sarcastically, ignoring his brother-in-law.

"Kevin?" Joanne gasped, shock evident in her expression. "What is wrong with you?" Pale, she sat down at the foot of the stairs.

Stratton knelt down and brushed a strand of her hair to one side. "Why don't you go on upstairs for a minute, hon?"

"I'm okay."

"But just a minute ago. . . ."

"I'm all right," Joanne insisted. "I want to know what happened with Kevin and Missy."

Kevin watched the exchange and immediately felt ashamed by his actions, as well as concerned for his sister. He stepped forward. "Joanne, what's the matter?" Belatedly he noticed that her face was chalky white and that her arms were folded around her stomach. "You sick?"

She shrugged in reply.

Stratton glanced at his wife, and after she nodded, he faced Kevin again. "She's got a miserable case of the stomach flu. She's been throwing up for the last four hours. That's why she's not on the third floor helping Missy."

Kevin felt like a board had hit him on the side of the head. "Oh."

Joanne gave him a wan smile. "I'm okay. I think it's almost over."

She was looking pale again. "Uh, isn't it supposed to last twenty-four hours or something?"

Stratton laughed. "Not necessarily. The flu hits everyone differently. In her case, I have a feeling it's going to be an all-night affair."

Joanne groaned. "What can I say? I'm special."

Stratton held out a hand and pulled Joanne up beside him. "You'll be okay, honey. You just need to go sip on a soda for a bit."

Kevin watched the two and felt their easy familiarity even from his distance. It was obvious that he was interrupting, and he was deeply embarrassed about his behavior. He closed his eyes briefly for a moment while he regrouped. "Hey, I'm really sorry," he said, shaking his head in confusion. "I don't know why I'm acting so crazy. I'll go ahead and leave. Sorry, Jo."

She stepped forward and grasped his arm. "No way, big brother. If Missy Schuler has you in such a dither, something big had to have happened. Come on in and tell us about it."

Kevin glanced at Stratton. The other man merely looked bemused.

"There's still an extra couple of roast beef sandwiches."

He was so hungry, anything sounded good. "Sold."

A few minutes later, he was dipping his kaiser roll into sauce and telling them about Missy. He explained how he had been trying to help her out, and then finally finished by recounting her blistering speech, and his departure from the Memorial Building. "I just don't get it, Joanne. I mean, she's got to know that I'm trying to help her. Why doesn't Missy see that? Why am I getting punished?"

"It sounds to me like she's just trying to develop her backbone," Stratton said.

"What?"

"I don't know her real well, but I do know from Joanne that she's had quite a few knocks in life, what with a single mom raising her, then a bad marriage. And she's had to make do with what she's had, which wasn't much. Now, with this job, and the dance, and that whole episode with the congressman, she's gaining confidence. I think she's trying to take control over her life. You ought to let her do that for a little bit."

"I'm not trying to take over her life; I'm just trying to help her out."

Joanne put down the saltine she was holding. "Kevin, I don't think she wants to be helped out by you."

"Well, what do you think she wants, then?"

"I think she wants you. Period. Not as some kind of rescuer, but as a boyfriend."

"That's what I said—and we've been doing that."

"No, I believe there's a difference, Kevin." Joanne sighed. "Remember last year, when I was dating Stratton, and I was doing all of those temp jobs. . . ."

Kevin grinned. "I remember."

"Well, I was so embarrassed to have to keep going to Stratton for help."

"I didn't mind," Stratton said.

She smiled at her husband. "I was not a good patient."

"Yeah, that bunny bite was tough to handle," Stratton quipped.

"Hush," she retorted. "Listen, Kevin. The only time I was able to feel good enough for Stratton was when I was feeling good about myself. You need to let Missy feel that way."

"I don't think your disastrous temp jobs are anything like Missy's problems."

"I happen to know that Missy's tougher than you think." Her eyes sparkled. "You should have heard Mom talking this afternoon about how impressed she is with Missy's handling of their meeting the other day."

"Really?"

Joanne nodded. "She told Mom and her buddies to get on track and toe the line."

He set his sandwich down. "What?"

"Well, she didn't say that in so many words . . . but she really did get them to listen. Mom thinks she's great."

Kevin took another bite of his sandwich while he considered her words. Maybe Joanne did have a point. "So what do you think I should do?"

"I think you should wait for her to make the next move, and I think you should put your coat of arms in the closet for a little bit. You don't have to be the white knight every day, Kevin. You can let other people tackle tough situations too."

"And you think if I do that, she'll come around?"

Joanne nodded. "I do. I know that she likes you a lot, Kevin."

Now that was something that he wanted to hear more about. "Really? She said so?"

"Yep. She's been awfully excited about your dates too. Plus, you are a good guy, once you settle down and don't try to solve everyone's problems."

"Thanks a lot," Kevin said sarcastically. "Stratton, help me out here."

"I would, if it seemed like you needed it." Stratton stretched his legs out in front of him. "Frankly, I have to admit that it just feels so good not to be the one trying to figure out a woman's mind right now."

"Hey." Joanne nudged him.

"I said trying, Jo. You know you're my enigma."

Kevin grinned at their silly exchange, then proceeded to get caught up on the latest news about Jeremy, Denise, and his parents. He couldn't help but grin when Joanne informed him that his parents had just signed up to be in a marlin fishing contest in Florida.

"But, they don't fish, Jo."

"I know that. You know that. But don't even think of telling Mom and Dad that they should reconsider . . . they're having too much fun getting outfitted with gear."

"When is this going to happen?"

"In a couple of weeks. A few days after the dance."

Stratton groaned when she mentioned the dance. "I have a feeling that this shindig is going to be a lot more trouble than anyone has counted on. You won't believe the outfit Joanne made for me."

"Oh, don't worry, Stratton," Joanne said sweetly. "I've already counted on it being a mini-nightmare. That's why I asked Missy to be in charge of it. It's always easier to tell someone else's mother and mother-in-law what to do."

Kevin felt nervous. "You think it's going to get that bad?"

Joanne laughed. "Of course, Kevin! But it will all

turn out all right. We just might all have migraines, sore muscles, and no patience by the time it comes, that's all."

Somehow, Kevin felt that those things were going to be the least of his problems.

Chapter Sixteen

As promised, Kevin called the next day. Missy held the phone warily as she spoke to him, wondering what he was going to say, and more importantly, how she would respond. But his first words took her completely off guard.

"I'm proud of you," he said quietly. "For what it's worth."

"What?"

"I'm glad you told me off. It did me a lot of good."

She tried to think of another time when she had spoken with less forethought and been praised so much. She responded slowly. "When did you decide this?"

"Right about the time Joanne finished giving me a piece of her mind . . . at about nine last night."

Missy sat down on her couch. "Joanne? You went over to her house?"

"Uh huh. I was so sure you needed taking care of . . . I was ready to tell Joanne off."

Something in his tone led her to believe that that wasn't quite how the conversation had transpired. "What happened?"

"First of all, Stratton set me straight on yelling at his wife."

She couldn't help but smile. "He didn't like that?"

"Nope. Especially not when she had been throwing up all afternoon."

"I guess not."

"Why didn't you tell me that she went home sick?"

"You didn't give me much of a chance. You weren't listening to anything I was saying. I guess you were just focused on your mission of mercy."

"More like a head trip, I think," Kevin said with a laugh. "I'm sorry."

"I forgive you."

He paused, then spoke again. "Missy, every time I think of you, I envision you soaked, sitting in my car, scared to death."

"There's more to me than that."

"I've found that out . . . and what I didn't, well Joanne filled me in."

She spoke slowly, not wanting to shake things up between them when they were just getting settled again. "Kevin, I don't know what I would have done without you that night. And your dates, your attention, they've been like nothing I've ever had before. I've probably enjoyed that spoiling too much."

"It wasn't spoiling. . . ."

"No, let me finish. I've been alone for a long time. When it was just my mother and I, I shouldered a lot of responsibility . . . and I had to be so tough when I was married to Scott." She leaned against the soft cushions of the couch, recalling just how hard her life had been. "Since then, I've had to subsist on less of everything: money . . . time . . . attention. The only thing I felt I could concentrate on was growing my savings account."

"I know that, Miss."

She smiled to herself ruefully. No he didn't. Kevin Reece had no idea what it had been like to do without so much for so long. "It was a big day in my life when I finally moved to my own place, and it's a long step away from your place."

"Missy. . . ."

"Listen. What I'm trying to tell you is that while I'm a strong person, I really enjoyed your attentions. I liked feeling fragile and soft. I probably encouraged your actions more than I should have . . . which is why I shouldn't have gotten so upset with you last night. You were just responding to my responses."

"I agree that you're resilient, Missy. But, I'll differ with you on my motivations. I've always been the type to shoulder things, to willingly take on other people's problems." He paused and then let out a deep chuckle. "Listen to us. Look, all I'm trying to tell you is that I want to be with you, just because of who you are."

It was impossible not to grin. "I feel the same way."

He sighed. "Then, we're okay?"

"I think we're just fine."

"You know, I realized after all of my posturing that I never even offered to help you last night. Are you working late tonight?"

"Yes."

"Would you like some help?"

"You bet, but I want to warn you that it's going to be crowded."

"Who's going to be there?"

"Your mom, Mrs. McKinley, their cohorts, your dad, Joanne, most of your family . . . we're going to decorate and put things up."

"That sounds like fun."

"Oh, it will be anything but." Missy laughed. "It's going to be chaos."

"Is there anything I can bring?"

"Yep. Come around six and bring some pizza and soda, and every trick you can think of to calm your mother and Joanne down."

"That's a tall order!"

"It's a dirty job, but someone has to do it."

"All right, I'll be there, armed with food, drinks, and a good attitude."

Missy smiled with pleasure. "I can't wait."

* * *

When he did arrive at 6:00 sharp, Missy wasn't sure whether to welcome him into the zoo, or beg him to take her away. For the last hour, people had been hammering, arguing, cleaning everything that didn't move, and—thanks to the Payton Band—blaring patriot songs in her ears. She didn't know how many more times she could hear the "Battle Hymn of the Republic" or "We'll Fight for Uncle Abe."

Daphne had taken over the hanging of the drapes with enough fanfare for a small awards ceremony. Every two minutes, she would hop off the ladder, pace back twenty steps, and ask if the curtains looked crooked.

Jim had decided to give everybody a break and be her official 'watcher,' so he stood directly in front of her, in the middle of the room, forcing everyone else to maneuver around his formidable frame.

Kevin strode into the middle of it all, looking calm and cool, as usual. Automatically she tried to catch his gaze, and caught her breath as she realized that at that moment, he didn't seem to be aware of anyone else but her.

His eyes looked icy gray and cool as they searched her face for any hints of how she was feeling. She met his own directly; attempting to convey without words how happy she was to see him.

Then, it was over, before the contact had really begun.

"Hey Kevin," Stratton called. "Come on in and grab a hammer. We're trying to get these old photos up before your mother changes her mind about where to hang them."

"I heard that," Daphne called out.

With an apologetic glance in her direction, Kevin gave his pizza boxes to Mary Beth and let himself be commandeered to the back of the room.

Then Missy didn't have time to worry about his actions because she and her clipboard were soon needed again. People pulled at her in all directions, and she tried her best to help each person.

During the next hour, she helped wash windows, placed tablecloths on side tables, and attempted to artfully arrange thirty flower arrangements. Joanne was keeping close tabs on her, and was once again fretting over a speech. She began tailing her around the room, reciting phrases and asking advice. Soon, Missy felt that she, too, had the speech memorized.

Kevin seemed just as busy. A couple of men had built a set of shelves and cabinets for the kitchen's back wall and needed help mounting them.

The tension in the room increased, and the noise got louder and louder. It seemed as if everyone was well aware that the party was just days away, and each felt responsible to get all of the work completed.

It took Mr. McKinley getting a nasty cut from a jagged edge of wood to calm everybody down. Although Baron looked more annoyed than anything else, Stratton patched him up and then suggested that it was time to call it a day.

Since it was almost midnight, Missy couldn't have agreed more. She was exhausted and frazzled from the commotion. After thanking everyone again for their help, she leaned back in a ladder-back chair and watched everyone leave in groups of two and three.

Finally it was just she, Joanne, Stratton, and Kevin.

"You look like you're about to faint," Stratton said, picking up yet another stray nail on the floor.

"I am. I don't know which tires me more, all of the work, or all of the noise," Missy admitted.

"It's *all* of it," Joanne replied. "It's the noise and the commotion . . . and the work, and the knowledge that it will all bc over in a few days' time." She looked at Stratton fondly. "Remember the two days before my museum opened?"

Stratton glanced at her fondly. "I do. I was practically standing guard over you . . . trying to get you to get some sleep."

Missy's eyes darted to Kevin, who said nothing, only looked at her with a knowing smile.

"Well, no matter what, I guess we better take Stratton's advice and call it a night," she said, standing up.

"You'll get no argument from me there," Joanne admitted. "After my bout with the flu yesterday, I'm exhausted." She looked from Kevin to Missy. "Are you guys coming too?"

"Sure," Kevin said. "I'll just help Missy lock up."

After saying good-bye to the other couple, Missy and Kevin made short work of locking up the room and turning out the lights. Finally they made their way down the long flights of stairs.

"I think I'm getting in pretty good shape, climbing up and down these stairs every day." Missy laughed.

"Me too." He held out his hand for her to take. "Wish I knew why the soldiers danced up here instead of on the first floor. It would have been easier on all of us if they hadn't."

"Maybe it's because when the soldiers were dancing up here, there was a mercantile on the first floor, and a hotel on the second."

Kevin chuckled at her matter-of-fact explanation. "I guess that's reason enough."

When they exited the building, Missy noticed that Kevin's car was parked directly behind hers. "I'm glad that you stopped by," she said as their footsteps slowed.

"Me too. Are you going straight here tomorrow?"

"Yes. With the dance in three days, I can't afford to do anything else."

"I'm almost afraid to ask this, but how about I give you a lift home?"

"I've got to be here early tomorrow morning."

"I'll pick you up early, and you can take me out to breakfast as a thank-you."

Silence hung in the air as she considered his words. Then, instinctively knowing that he offered just to be with her, not to do yet another good deed, she accepted. "Thanks. I'd like that very much."

Missy leaned back in the soft leather gratefully and relaxed. Between the emotional roller coaster of the day before and the physical labor that she had been doing, she was utterly exhausted. In spite of herself, she yawned. "This is nice."

Kevin reached over to take her hand. "It is," he said quietly, then drove the few miles to her home in silence. This was what he had been looking for all of his life; someone to sit quietly with, not to have to entertain or amuse.

Kevin distractedly rubbed the top of her hand with his thumb. As he turned the corner to her street, he spoke again. "I was thinking that when all of this was over, it would be nice to get out of town for a day. Have you been to Amish country much?"

No answer.

"Well, it's a nice drive; the countryside's very pretty. There's quite a few shops to visit also. We could stop somewhere, have lunch, just enjoy the outdoors."

He paused again, then continued when she didn't speak. "I know that next week it will be April and still a little chilly, but the weatherman said that we were due for a little heat wave. So, what do you think? Missy?"

Finally he glanced at her. Missy had her head tilted

back against the seat and was sleeping soundly. He belatedly realized that her hand hung limply in his. After driving the last five minutes in silence, he parked the car, then turned to her, amused. "Miss?" he whispered, "Missy, wake up."

She only curled her body closer to his. The action sent a tremor through his whole body. Visions of Missy, sleeping next to him, sharing his bed every day, came to mind. The temptation to touch her was strong. Gently, he reached out and ran his fingers along the strands of hair that cascaded across her shoulder. Then, he traced the planes of her cheek, the line of her jaw. Her skin felt warm and supple. Finally, he couldn't help himself. He leaned down and kissed her gently. Then again.

Her eyes drifted open, then widened as she saw his face just inches from hers. "Did I fall asleep?" she mumbled.

"You did."

She looked dismayed. "I'm sorry. . . ."

"Don't be. It was kind of fun to play Prince Charming to your Sleeping Beauty."

He was delighted to see an amused expression cross her features as she sat up and gathered her belongings. "It was kind of fun to wake up this way."

He thought so too. He could imagine performing that task every morning for the rest of their lives.

And that's what he thought about when he finally made his way back home, at a quarter to one in the morning.

Chapter Seventeen

"A couple of things to keep in mind for next time," Joanne mumbled three days later as she sidled over to Missy, her pale green hoopskirts brushing against Missy's blue ones. "Number one: Never plan a Civil War dance when there is a chance of rain or sleet."

"We could not have predicted the spring storm."

"Everyone's hair is plastered to their head."

"They'll survive."

"And the costumes. . . ." Joanne arched an auburn eyebrow. "Everyone's costumes are ruined. Did you see how those ladies attempted to keep warm and dry in those coats? They all looked like sausages, wrapped up too tight."

It was not a good image. "They didn't look that bad."

Joanne harrumphed. "Next time, we plan the party for summer."

"You never know how it could be then," Missy stated, playing the devil's advocate for fun. "In the middle of summer, it could be worse; it could be a hundred degrees outside. We'd be awfully hot, or there could be a tornado!"

Joanne ignored her. "Number two: Next time we decide to redecorate a building and host a party, let's plan to have it on the first floor, so everyone isn't trying to squeeze up the narrow staircase in hoop-skirts."

"But this is exactly the spot where the original dances were held," Missy admonished her. "That's what is supposed to be so charming!"

Joanne bit her lip. "We could just keep that as our little secret."

Missy couldn't even fathom what to say to that. Poor Joanne really was beside herself with nerves.

"Number three: Say loudly that I don't have to be a featured speaker." Joanne shook her head in dismay. "It's hard enough to sound knowledgeable, but almost impossible with cleavage showing, dressed in the color of lime sherbet, and afraid to move my head."

Missy looked again at Joanne's beautiful hairdo. A few of the beauty shops in town had gotten into the spirit and had offered to arrange the ladies' hair in elaborate coiffures reminiscent of the time period. Joanne's hair was a mass of expertly pinned ringlets, with pearls and peridot-colored stones scattered through it. She probably also had the contents of a can of hair spray in it to hold it in place. "Your hair is lovely, Joanne. And you'll do a great job speaking. You always do."

But her boss didn't seem to want to hear any praise. Instead, she held out another glove-covered finger and spoke. "Number four."

"Oh, Joanne. Enough!" Missy giggled, then stopped in surprise at her words. Wow, she really had gotten brave.

"Limit the number of guests."

"I believe we only sent out two hundred invitations."

"I think those two hundred each brought two friends. It's packed!"

"Think of how much lemonade you're going to sell."

Joanne's laugh turned into a groan as she scanned the crowd. "And finally, number five: No matter what we do, leave Payton Chase off of the guest list."

Missy grimaced. Joanne did have a point there. "You know that we had to invite him, Joanne. He was one of our biggest supporters!"

Joanne's eyes narrowed as she gazed at Payton Chase. "Still. . . ."

Seeing that Joanne had spotted her target, Missy cast a glance at him also, and grinned when she found him. There was Joanne's ex-boyfriend near the punch bowl. His blond hair was slicked back and his signet pinky ring was glimmering as he chatted with the mayor and council members. He was dressed in an old-fashioned suit and teal-colored vest, and he looked as attractive as ever.

It was really too bad that he and Joanne had had such a falling-out. She'd heard that he'd had a change of ways and had abandoned his family business in order to take over the management of the Payton Country Club. He was actually working hard and making sound decisions. And, for the first time in a while, he was garnering respect.

They were prevented from further conversation by a rousing rendition of "When Johnny Comes Marching Home," played with enough gusto by the Payton High School band that they could have been heard from the top bleacher at the football field. A dozen men dressed as Ulysses S. Grant were lined up together, swaying in time to the beat.

Other people had gotten into the spirit and were either saluting the flags or singing along. Personally, Missy couldn't have hoped for a better crowd.

Actually, all in all, she was as pleased as could be with the whole production. The room was beautiful, the music was enthusiastic, and everyone was excited to be there and show off their costumes. A few people had even adopted Southern accents to go with their traditional garb, not seeming to care that they were supposed to be acting as if they were on the Northern side.

And she had made more friends than she could count while working on the project. Ladies now stopped her in the coffee shop or grocery store and asked how she was doing. Mrs. Reece had taken her to some favorite spots to shop for discount furnishings, and she would always look back on that afternoon when they made the curtains together with fondness.

There was only one person who she hoped to see this evening though—Kevin. More than anything she wanted him to see the fruition of all of her hard work. Carefully, she scanned the crowd, hoping to catch his eye.

And there he finally was, looking debonair and handsome as could be in a black cutaway jacket and burgundy colored vest. He had even slicked back his hair with some kind of oil. He looked suave and strange and irresistible as he strode toward her.

"How're you doing?" he asked.

Missy motioned her head in the direction of his sister. "Hanging in there. Joanne's been having a few last-minute jitters."

"And you? You look lovely all dolled up like a Southern belle."

She gave a mock curtsy. "Thank you kindly," she said. Privately, she did have to admit that she liked her periwinkle dress with the yellow rosettes very much, as well as her own intricate coiffure. Joanne and the other ladies had presented the dress and gift certificate the night before as a thank-you present. She felt like a true Civil War–era lady. "I just hope everything goes all right tonight."

Kevin looked around him. Groups of people stood near the bar, the band, and along the tables on the sides. Several surrounded Congressman Zeiler, who had dandified himself up nicely and looked as if he was perfectly at home in his old-fashioned garb. He was giving out cards and shaking hands.

Others were standing near the entryway, greeting a large group who had just arrived. The chatter was noisy, but genial. Things did seem to be going well.

The band began to play "Waltz Across Texas," adding to the feeling of unity in the room. A slow smile lit Kevin's features. "You care to give it a try?"

"What?"

"Waltzing in your skirts."

"Oh, I don't know."

"Come on—it'll be fun."

So, slowly, they entered the dance floor. Missy held on as Kevin led her through the motions of the dance. "I didn't know that you knew how to dance," she said, more for something to say than anything.

"I happen to have a whole wealth of talents that you've only just glimpsed," he quipped.

"Lucky me."

She laughed as Kevin spun her, and finally had a chance to truly take in his beautiful attire. He looked every inch the successful Victorian businessman, with vest, long coat, and striped wool pants. An unlit cigar was in his chest pocket. An oh-so-loving expression played on his lips. They called to her. Not caring about anyone else in the room, she leaned forward and kissed him. And, to her surprise, his hands immediately grasped her waist and held on as he eagerly kissed her back.

They twirled and circled the floor again, then broke apart as the congressman himself claimed her hand.

From that point on, her night became a blur. Missy chatted with the other volunteer women, and danced with anyone and everyone who asked her. She drank lemonade and manned the refreshment table. She clapped for the band and organized everyone to listen to Joanne's speech. But most of all, she reveled in the fact that she was there at all. Somewhere in between the time when she had run out of gas on the highway, and that very minute, she had come out of her shell. It made her feel proud and substantial.

It was a wonderful night. She leaned toward Kevin to tell him so, but was prevented when a clap of thunder echoed in the distance, and the lights flickered. Missy pulled back from Kevin. "Uh-oh."

"Uh-oh, what?"

She couldn't help but laugh nervously. "I think the power is about to go out. You better be near Joanne to catch her when she faints."

Genuine alarm crossed his features. "Why do you say that?"

"If the lights go out after all of the trouble that we went to, it's going to send her over the edge."

Several people gasped when the lights flickered again, but otherwise it didn't seem to dampen anyone's mood. Missy heard a few people make good-natured remarks about searching for candles.

The thunder cracked again, but this time the crash was followed by an intake of breath from one of the ladies who had worked so hard with Missy to make the curtains. "Oh, no," she cried.

Complete silence answered her call.

Even from where Missy stood in the corner, she could hear Joanne run over to the woman to see the problem. And then, all eyes looked up.

A drip had begun right over the buffet line. Missy added her groan to the chorus of others when she saw where it came from.

A large patch about the size of a plate had formed over the chafing dishes of Italian meatballs. The paint had bubbled and condensation had formed. A two-inch-wide fissure in the center seemed particularly troublesome. The ceiling looked like it was about to give way at any time.

Frantically, Missy wondered how people would take it if the ceiling began to fall on the noisy crowd, just like Chicken Little, but she didn't have a chance to find out, because the lights flickered one last time and finally died.

Groans rose up, followed by a high-pitched squeal or two. Then finally—like a grand finale—a loud splat. "There go the meatballs!" someone shouted.

Missy shook her head in despair. Laughter and commotion erupted again.

And then she heard one voice, unmistakably standing out from all of the rest. "Add this to my list, Missy!"

"I already have," Missy called out, laughing.

Chapter Eighteen

The big question of the night was a simple one: Was a party a success if you had close to 300 people stranded in a small room, in the dark? With plaster from an ill-repaired ceiling falling on them as well as most of the food? When the only way out was down three narrow flights of stairs? With most women wearing cumbersome dresses, and several men all looking alike, thanks to an inordinate fondness for Ulysses S. Grant?

Missy didn't know.

How about the rain? Could that count against her also? Especially with the rainfall in the room becoming increasingly steady. Again, it was up to the fates to decide.

What was she going to do to save the party?

She bit her lip. When things like this happened, did people automatically want their money back? Did United States congressmen frown terribly upon botched extravaganzas like this?

Shadows moved in front of her, and then became illuminated, thanks to Daphne and Marianne's forethought in providing candle lanterns for each table. Baron McKinley was currently using his Zippo lighter to light each one, along with one of his ever-present cigars. Occupants at each table greeted him with the fanfare of a returning hero, and clapped him on the back as he lit each candle.

Missy said a small prayer of thanks for Baron. She had no idea if anyone had had the forethought to provide emergency flashlights. But at present, it didn't seem to matter; the candlelight had given the room a warm, romantic glow, illuminating everyone's faces in a calming radiance. An aromatic freesia scent wafted through the air mixed with Baron's cigar smoke.

Outside, another clap of thunder reverberated. She knew it would be best to begin herding everyone out the door and down the narrow passageway. And surely the first person should be their congressman?

Missy looked warily for her honored guest, the distinguished Congressman Zeiler, then let out a sigh of relief. He wore a grin and it looked as if he had managed to pilfer one of Baron McKinley's cigars. He seemed quite content to have his cocktail at one of the back tables while charming the ladies' guild with another story about Washington insiders.

In fact, the party had continued in spite of all of the problems, Missy realized in wonder. If anything, the crowd had relaxed somewhat and now seemed intent on enjoying themselves as much as possible instead of worrying about the state of their costumes.

As if on cue, the band began to play "Twist and Shout," and couples started doing just that in every available space. All of those hoop skirts in motion were surely a sight to behold, Missy mused.

Someone had moved the meatballs and set an empty tin container to catch the drips from the ceiling. She heard laughter from the mayor and his wife as they talked with Joanne and Stratton, and wonder of wonders, the band next played a medley of sixties' show tunes, for which they showed a remarkable aptitude.

Finally she looked to Kevin, who was chatting with a group of people from his country club. He also acted as if the building's tribulations were only minor inconveniences.

What was it with these people? Didn't they realize that practically everything that could have gone wrong had? That the night was a disaster even though she had put hours into planning, organizing, and decorating the old place? Suddenly the irony of it all became too much. Wearily Missy sat down on an available chair. This had to be the craziest night of her life.

"It's pretty wild in here, isn't it?" Daphne said as

she approached and expertly positioned herself in a chair next to Missy.

"It is something else," Missy agreed. "I can't believe how well everyone is taking it. I thought for sure that by now Joanne would have fainted or I would be besieged with people asking for their money back."

Daphne tilted her head, amused. "You may be surprised by everyone's lack of theatrics. In spite of the dim light and indoor rain, it's been a perfect party."

They sat in silence for a few moments, each content to watch the scene unfold in front of them. Mary Beth and Cameron were slow dancing, groups of people were mingling at the bar, and Joanne and Stratton seemed to be in deep conversation in the back of the room.

Little by little, people began to leave the party. Coats were retrieved, umbrellas claimed, and thanks relayed. Then, as if by mutual agreement, the partiers left in groups of ten or twelve, taking a table votive to guide their way.

After a while, Kevin joined his mother and Missy. "This was a great party, ladies," he said debonairly.

"Thank you very much, sweetie," Daphne answered smugly. "I had several people from bridge tell me that this was the most fun they'd had in years."

"Since Founder's Day in '84," Jim added as he wandered over.

Daphne nodded. "That was a good party."

"I just don't know how we're going to top this next

year, Miss," Joanne said as she and Stratton approached. "We'll have to go back to the research books to find some more interesting historical landmarks."

Missy groaned at the thought of another party to plan. She looked from one Reece member to the other. They acted as if crazy get-togethers were commonplace. "I don't know, Joanne. I think perhaps we ought to make parties like this an every-other-year affair."

Joanne looked crestfallen. "But I already told everybody to plan on it, same time next year. Congressman Zeiler is going to bring friends!" She crossed her arms in front of her chest. "We'll figure it out. Once the electricity gets fixed, everything will be a piece of cake."

Missy couldn't help it; she started to laugh. "All right. After all, you are the boss."

"Don't worry, Missy," Stratton teased. "In a few years, events like this will seem normal."

After some discussion, the Reece family decided to give Missy a break, and Kevin volunteered to take her home. For once, Missy didn't mind leaving her responsibilities one bit. She was tired and as confused as ever about her relationship with Kevin's family. They all spoke as if she was going to be around for a long time . . . but as what? Joanne's friend? Kevin's girlfriend? Daphne's party planner?

Once she and Kevin were in his car, she couldn't resist stating the obvious. "Well, here we are again."

He smiled. “Yep. It’s good I like to drive you around, huh?”

She smiled. “Did you realize that it’s been almost a month since I was stranded on the freeway?”

“I do, but to be honest, it feels like much longer. I can’t imagine my days without you now.”

His words brought a fresh burst of joy. “Really?”

He maneuvered the car out of the parking lot, then clasped her hand. “Really. I think that there’s something pretty special between us. We get along well together.”

Missy glanced down at their intertwined hands. Kevin’s looked so strong and sure beside hers. “I think so too.”

He glanced at her quickly. “Do you ever think about us?”

How honest did she want to be? “Yes.”

“I’ve been thinking about us quite a bit, actually,” he said thoughtfully. “You know, it’s funny, but things in my life are just better when you’re around.”

“How so?”

“I remember to appreciate going to the movies, and eating breakfast with my mom. I look forward to the weekends . . . and having a really good cup of coffee.” He darted a glance in her direction. “You make everything glow, Missy.”

She squeezed his hand. “I feel the same way about you.”

That brought a smile to his face. “That’s good. I,

uh, have been thinking that one day. . . ." His voice drifted off as he parked in front of her house and then twisted in his seat to face her.

Her heart felt as if it couldn't beat fast enough. "Yes?"

"One day. . . ." Kevin coughed once. "Well . . . I don't want to rush you or anything. . . ."

She couldn't stand it. "Yes, Kevin?" she prompted, with an edge to her words.

He looked uncomfortable. "I was thinking—no, hoping," he amended, "that one day you might want to get married again?"

"Again?"

He looked straight ahead, as if he couldn't trust his expression. "You know, when you're ready?"

Her eyes widened. Was this what she thought it was? She pulled her hands out of his grasp and placed them on his forearms. "Kevin, are you asking me to marry you?"

He closed his eyes for a moment, then finally nodded. "Yes, I'm very clumsily asking you to marry me, one day . . . in a couple of months . . . or years . . . um, when you feel ready."

He looked so serious, she couldn't help but smile. "You want to wait years?"

The corners of his lips twitched. "Actually, that wouldn't be my first choice."

Her voice softened. "I have a pretty good idea about when I might want to get married again."

"When?"

"When the man I want to marry loves me as much as I love him."

His eyes searched her face, as if he were trying to read her thoughts. "I love you now," he rasped.

"And I love you back," she said with confidence. Finally, she knew where she belonged. Right here. With Kevin Reece.

He gently folded her into his arms. And once again, Missy knew that it was where she was meant to be.

Epilogue

Months later, Missy stood at the back of the church, watching her bridesmaids make their way down the aisle in front of her. Both Mary Beth and Joanne looked especially pretty in the soft pink sheaths. The dresses complimented the large bouquets of carnations, roses, and gardenias that lined the altar and the pews.

As she fingered the thick satin fabric of her wedding gown, she thought of how different this was from her first wedding. Where before she had stood in front of the justice of the peace, she was now in a beautiful church, built at the turn of the century. The first time there had only been herself and Scott—now almost a hundred people were in attendance. Before, she had felt frightened and nervous—now, she only felt calm and excited.

And, of course, this time, she was marrying Kevin.

Violinists were playing the last strains of "Ave Maria." The scent of gardenias seemed to hang in the humid July air. Missy breathed in, knowing that she would remember that sweet scent the rest of her life.

Finally she turned to the distinguished gentleman beside her.

"You hanging in there?" Congressman Zeiler asked good-naturedly.

"Just about."

"Good." The congressman's elbow was already propped up—ready to take her hand and lead Missy down the aisle and into the next stage of her life.

"I'm so glad you're here, and walking me down the aisle," she said, still unable to believe that he had offered to be with her in this special way.

The whole day simply felt like a dream. Imagine she, Missy Schuler, being walked down the aisle of a grand church on the arm of a United States congressman! With people that she loved in attendance, and beautiful music playing in the background. It was so amazing. A warm feeling of happiness floated through her.

Congressman Zeiler looked as proud as a peacock. "I told you, I only do the aisle thing for people who save my life," he teased.

She raised her eyebrows. "But you already attended the dance. . . ."

"Which was for the town and the community." He finished her sentence. "This, my dear, is for you."

Just then, the beginning chords of "The Wedding March" echoed through the sanctuary. Missy peeked through the curtains. The pianist played a flowing introduction, and the whole congregation stood up.

"We better start walking." The Congressman chuckled, peeking through the doorway. "I don't believe Kevin has taken his eyes off this spot for a minute, he's so eager for you to appear."

Missy stepped forward and took his arm. "Then I better do just that."

The curtains parted, and Missy smiled as the crowd drew in a collective breath.

"Congratulations, Missy Reece," Congressman Zeiler murmured as they began their trek up the aisle in measured steps.

"Thank you," she answered breathlessly as she turned her head to meet Kevin's warm gaze. His eyes looked luminescent as they met her own. Then slowly, he smiled.

Yes, she had finally found a love to last a lifetime . . . a love to hold forever.